THE ROAD TO AMAZING

TO AMAZING

BRENT HARTINGER

BOOKS

Song: "This Time and Place"
Words by Brent Hartinger,
Music by Brent Hartinger and Danny Oryshchyn

BK Books
www.brenthartinger.com

Cover design by Philip Malaczewski

ISBN-13: 978-1523418046

For Michael Jensen

And for everyone who fought for
marriage equality—
talk about a leap of faith!

CHAPTER ONE

I'd come to the end of the gravel road. If I went any farther, I'd drive straight into Puget Sound.

"This is wrong," I said to my boyfriend Kevin, sitting next to me in the car. "It's another dead end."

"We're going to be late," he said. "We need to call and tell that Christie woman." He looked at the clock on the dash of our rental car. "Oh, geez, we're *already* late."

"No, wait," I said, spotting something through the pine trees on our left. "I think that's it."

It was early evening, right after sunset, but through the trunks of those trees, I'd seen the vague outline of a house. It was grey, and long and angular, like a collection of boxes all spread out and askew, perched at the edge of a cliff and looking over the water. It was called the Amazing Inn, but it wasn't an actual inn, with a desk clerk or a bellhop or anything like that. It was just a big house you could rent for the weekend. There wasn't even a sign outside.

"Finally," Kevin said, even as he sat stiffly in his seat.

The Amazing Inn was located on Vashon Island in the middle of Puget Sound in Washington State. To the northeast of the island was the city of Seattle, and Tacoma was located directly to the south. I read somewhere that Vashon Island was surrounded by some three million people—all the people crowded into those cities on the mainland—so naturally you'd expect the island itself to be crowded too. But it wasn't: there were only a few thousand people on what was actually a pretty big piece of land. Every time the state had proposed building a bridge, the islanders had revolted.

And so, despite being so close to everything, at least as the seagull flies, Vashon Island was hard to get to. As a result, it felt a little bit like a world apart, a place out of time, with woods and farmlands and rolling hills. But it didn't feel "rural" exactly either, because it didn't have that redneck-y vibe, with trailer parks and Bible verses posted everywhere. On the contrary, the island was covered with organic farms, and artists' studios, and funky little coffee houses.

In short, Vashon Island was a cross between Burning Man and *Anne of Green Gables.*

The part we were on, the upper west side of the island, was especially empty. It was probably because of all the steep hills and twisty roads. The forests grew really thick here, and there weren't very many houses. The ones that were here, like the Amazing Inn, were built atop cliffs right above the beaches and coves, and tucked away at the end of long, winding, gravel roads.

It was funny, because Kevin and I had been to this exact spot once before, a couple of months earlier, when we'd decided to rent this house in the first place. It hadn't seemed so hard to find then, but that had been in daylight. Now it was late on a Friday at the end of

September, and the lights in the house were all off, which was why it had been so hard to see.

"We should send out an email," Kevin said. "Tell everyone it's hard to find."

"Yeah, maybe," I said.

We sat there for a second, then Kevin said, "So where *is* she? Maybe she already came and left."

He meant Christie, the person who'd showed us the house before. Now she was meeting us to hand off the key, and also take us on a final walkthrough. Unlike a real inn, there wasn't anyone living on-site, so we were going to have the complete run of the place all weekend long.

I glanced at the clock. "We're fifteen minutes late," I said. "I can't believe she wouldn't wait fifteen minutes."

"But what do we do if she doesn't show up?"

"I guess we could send out an email about that too. 'Don't come, the ceremony's been canceled.'"

Kevin didn't laugh, not even a smile. He was nervous, not just about our being late, but about the whole weekend. And, well, it was also a really stupid joke.

I guess I'm sort of burying the real story. Kevin and I were getting married. That's why we'd rented this house for the weekend. The actual ceremony was taking place in two days, on Sunday afternoon—sixty-seven guests in all. But we'd invited our closest friends to join us here for the two days before, partly to get everything ready, but also because we wanted to celebrate.

Why didn't I mention this until now? It's not because I was dreading the wedding—that I had serious doubts, or last-minute jitters, or anything like that. That's also not why I made that stupid joke about canceling the wedding.

Kevin didn't have any doubts either. I was sure that's not why he was nervous.

He and I met when we were sixteen. We connected online first, then in person in a park at night (probably not the best choice on my part, but hey, it worked out in the end). He ended up being my first romance. We'd been on and off again for a long time after that, but then two years earlier, we'd gotten together for good. We'd gone through some difficult times, and also some really good ones. In the end, I'd been the one to propose, and he'd accepted without hesitation.

The time had been so right. And ever since that proposal, I hadn't doubted for one second that it was exactly the right thing to do.

I wanted to marry Kevin, and I was certain he wanted to marry me.

It's funny, because contrary to what the religious nutjobs tell you, I think gay guys like weddings more than anyone. And it isn't that we're mocking the institution of marriage, or because we want to destroy it all to hell. It's because we really, really want to get married.

What a concept, huh?

It makes sense when you think about it. Almost every older gay person alive today has been told most of their lives: "You don't fit in! You're not good enough for marriage! You can't have a star on your belly!"

For a while, that made a lot of gay people (understandably) angry and offended. "To hell with you!" a lot of us said. "We didn't want to be part of your stupid old institution of marriage anyway!"

But then society changed. It said, "Okay, we've changed our minds. I guess we'll let you get married after all. You can totally thank us now."

Some gay people were still pretty bitter about this, especially the older ones who had to put up with a lot more shit than the rest of us. And every gay person, except maybe the gay Republicans, was at least a little annoyed by this expectation that we were supposed to be so incredibly grateful that society was finally treating us the way we should have been treated all along, like they were somehow doing us this *huge* favor.

But despite some lingering bitterness, most of us gay folk went running straight for the elaborate wedding cakes and flash-mob wedding proposals. "Yay!" we said. "Now we can have stars on our bellies too!"

When it comes right down to it, a lot of us gay guys are romantics at heart. You can take us out of a Broadway musical, but you can't take the Broadway musical out of us. (Yes, yes, I'm stereotyping shamelessly. But come on.)

With my entire being, I wanted to marry Kevin Land, and I was just as certain that he wanted to marry me too.

Headlights appeared behind us, tires crunching on the gravel road.

"Here we go," Kevin said, turning for the car door. We both stepped out into the little parking area, which was also sort of a cul-de-sac.

The other car parked next to ours, and a woman climbed out—Christie, the person we'd met before. She was this slight Asian woman, a little like a hummingbird, simultaneously no-nonsense and a little bit flighty.

"Sorry!" she said. "Sorry I'm late! I'm so, so sorry!"

I was about to tell her that she didn't have anything to worry about, that we'd been late too, and only arrived a minute or two before she did, but she didn't give me a chance.

"Really, I'm sorry!" she went on. "Just so sorry."

She'd given us about four more "sorrys" than was necessary. In ten seconds, she'd gone from being sympathetic to annoying.

I looked at Kevin, both of us rolling our eyes a little behind her back.

"Don't worry about it," I said to Christie.

"It's fine," Kevin said. "Can we look at the house now?"

We grabbed our suitcases from the car, and Christie led us to the big grey house, apologizing a couple more times along the way.

"Oh!" she said when we reached the front door. "You're the ones who are getting married, aren't you?"

"Yeah," Kevin said, "that's us."

"That's so great! Congratulations, I'm so happy for you."

Maybe Christie was this happy about all the couples who rented her house for their weddings, but I think part of it was that Kevin and I were a gay couple. And can I just say? Out of all the people we'd dealt with over our wedding—caterers, gift registry people, the clerk at city hall—not a single person had acted weird about the fact that we were two guys. On the contrary, a lot of people had acted like Christie, excited by the semi-novelty of it all.

I can't tell you what a nice surprise this was, especially after all the bullshit you hear about the horrors of gay marriage from politicians and conservative Christians.

"Where are you going on your honeymoon?" Christie asked us.

"We're not going on one," I said. "We couldn't really afford it. Maybe next year."

"Oh, I'm sorry!" Christie said. "I'm really sorry."

"It's okay," I said, and behind her back, Kevin and I smiled at each other again over her new string of apologies.

The truth is, this time Christie sort of *had* done something wrong—though not something she had to apologize for. Kevin and I couldn't afford a honeymoon, and it sucked to be reminded of that. Hell, we could barely afford this wedding. The year before, we'd moved from Seattle to Los Angeles, and now I worked as a barista, trying to make it as a screenwriter, and Kevin did freelance writing and editing for IMDb. So to save money, we'd moved the wedding from summer to fall (when the rates were cheaper), and we'd given up on the idea of a honeymoon entirely, even a weekend away.

Inside the Amazing Inn, Christie turned on the lights, and it was just as great as I remembered. The house wasn't new exactly, but still modern. It was all one floor, with lots of angles and lines, and sunken steps, and huge picture windows that looked out over the water—up toward Blake Island to the north and down toward Point Richmond on the opposite side of Puget Sound. Somehow the house was bold and interesting, but unobtrusive, a beautiful picture frame outlining the sweeping water view. Just outside, the house also had a massive wrap-around deck.

The main room was by far the biggest, with a high ceiling and open area that flowed into the kitchen and the dining room, off to one side. The plan was for our wedding ceremony to take place out on the deck, which was (hopefully) big enough for sixty-seven people, but we also had this large inside room in case it rained.

We couldn't afford a honeymoon, it's true, but we'd managed to find a pretty fantastic wedding venue. That made me happy, and Kevin was smiling too.

Christie had shown us the house once before, months earlier, but now she went over the basics: what not to put down the garbage disposal, where the extra toilet paper was stored, stuff like that.

When she was showing us the gas fire pit out on the deck, she stopped and said, "Oh, I'm sorry, I hope I didn't forget to ask. There aren't any kids staying this weekend, are there?"

"No," Kevin said. "No kids."

Was it my imagination or did Kevin sound kind of wistful?

Honestly, this was another thing about the wedding, sort of a disagreement between us. Remember what I said before about gay guys all wanting to get married? Well, a lot of gay guys don't just want to get married— they want to *get married*. They want the whole kit and caboodle. (Does anyone say "kit and caboodle" anymore? Did anyone *ever* say "kit and caboodle"?).

They want to cuddle in front of the TV, hate-watching *American Horror Story*. They want Thursday game nights, and Saturday dinner parties, and Sunday trips to Costco. They want a dog, and a late-night health club, and a house with a yard (but not a house in the suburbs, because, come on, gay guys aren't *crazy*).

And kids. It suddenly seemed like every gay guy I'd ever met was talking about having kids.

I don't want kids.

Some people say, "Never say never! You never know!"

But I'll say it:

I. Will. Never. Want. Kids.

I don't want to offend anyone, so I'll leave aside all the talk about how kids are shrill and stinky, and how most parents talk about nothing except how amazing their shrill and stinky kids are (and how, thanks to their kids, they never get enough sleep).

The point is, I had all these plans for my life, things I wanted to do, that would simply have been impossible with kids in the picture.

I was never shy about this opinion with Kevin. He was pretty clear with his feelings too: that he didn't know for sure, but yeah, he probably wanted kids someday. So before we planned the wedding, we sat down and talked it all out. Basically, I said, "I'm never going to want kids. Are you okay with that?" Because kids aren't really something you can compromise on.

In the end, Kevin had said, "Russel, it's fine. Being with you is more important than having kids. Kids weren't that big a deal to me anyway."

It was great to hear, but even now, months after we'd had that conversation, I wondered if it was really true.

Later, Kevin stayed in the house unpacking, and I walked Christie to her car.

"Thanks for everything," I said. "This place really is amazing."

"Oh, that's not why we call it the Amazing Inn."

"What?"

"It's named after the town. Amazing, Washington."

"Yeah?" I'd lived in Washington State most of my life, and I'd never heard that name before. "Where's Amazing?"

"Well, it doesn't exist anymore. But it did, years ago. Right here."

"Wow," I said, only mildly curious. I wanted to get back inside the house and check out the Jacuzzi tub in the master bedroom.

"Sorry, not *here* exactly." She gestured toward some trees on the opposite side of the road. "There. You can see ruins and everything."

I looked over my shoulder.

It turns out I'd been wrong: the road hadn't ended where I thought. Just up from the parking area, another dirt road headed off into the forest. But it was so over-grown that I'd missed it, or maybe I'd assumed it was only another driveway.

"Ruins?" I said.

"Well, not ruins-ruins. Just some foundations and an abandoned well. I'm sorry, did I ask you if there are going to be any kids staying here this weekend?"

"Yes," I said. "And no, no kids. Absolutely no kids!"

"Oh, I'm sorry," Christie said, and I felt bad I'd sort of snapped at her.

"When was all this?" I said, lowering my voice. "When was there a town here?"

"Turn of the last century. Amazing was one of the stops on the Mosquito Fleet. Just a small place, really."

Puget Sound was a long, complicated series of bays and waterways, and back before they built good roads to connect all the cities and towns on the sound, people used boats to get around. There had even been this circuit of private steamboats that ran up and down

Puget Sound, stopping at each dock. Because this was the main source of transportation, towns grew around those docks. Later, the roads got better, and people started driving cars, so the Mosquito Fleet was replaced by the Washington State Ferry System, which had boats big enough to carry cars. But it wasn't the same thing. The Washington State ferries only stopped at ferry landings, and there was usually only one landing per island.

"So Amazing disappeared when the Mosquito Fleet faded away, huh?" I said, feeling a little pleased with myself that I knew as much as I did about local history.

But Christie shook her head. "No. It was years before that."

"Yeah? What happened?"

"No one knows."

I looked at her skeptically.

"It's true!" she said. "Apparently, one day the whole town simply vanished. The people, I mean, not the buildings. There were only twenty-six people total. One day they were here, and the next day when the steamboat arrived, they were all gone."

"That's crazy. Someone must know where they went."

Assuming it's even true that the people vanished in the first place, I thought.

"No," she said. "People have studied it. Every few years, a reporter writes an article about it for the *Seattle Times*, or does a piece for one of the local TV stations. A team of historians came out here once—stayed at the inn almost two weeks. Everyone thinks they can solve the mystery of Amazing, Washington, but no one ever does." Christie fumbled for her keys.

I looked back over toward the road to Amazing. It still wasn't completely dark outside, but it was funny how quickly the road disappeared into the trees. I swear I couldn't see more than five feet down it.

I'd been bored with her story at first, but I wasn't anymore. I mean, come on, who doesn't love a mystery?

"What do *you* think happened?" I asked.

She found the keys in her purse and looked up at me. "What?"

"To the people of Amazing."

She looked over at the road, even as she seemed to draw in on herself, like a vole ducking out of sight from a raptor.

"What?" I said.

"Nothing."

"No, seriously. I want to know."

Clutching her keys, she stared at me.

"Aliens," she said at last.

I laughed before I realized that she hadn't been kidding.

"Really?" I said.

She nodded at me with wide eyes. Then she lowered her voice, as if someone was going to hear us way out in the woods of Vashon Island, or cared about alien conspiracies anyway. "This guy came and stayed here once, and he told me all about it. They look for places like Amazing—remote, isolated towns. And they *observe*, sometimes for years. Then one day it happens: the people disappear! Aliens did the same thing to that colony on Roanoke Island in Virginia back in the sixteenth century."

At this point, I was thinking: *Have Kevin and I really rented a house for the weekend from a crazy person?* What if this wasn't even her house? Maybe her angel-guide had told her she had permission to start renting out the neighbor's house as her own.

"Some people think the aliens build re-creations of these remote little towns on their spaceships," she went on, "so when they're finally abducted, the people don't even know it! The people of Amazing might still exist, their descendants anyway, living on some alien space-craft!"

I was back to being bored with Christie, and also a little nervous that she might suddenly pull a knife on me, so I said, "That's really interesting. Anyway, well, thanks for everything! We'll leave the key where you told us."

I think she heard the dismissive, freaked-out tone in my voice, and I felt guilty again. I mean, I'd been the one to drag it out of her. Who was I to make fun of her beliefs?

But she got my message. She exaggerated a nod and starting climbing into her car.

Now I felt like I sort of owed *her* an apology.

"I mean, maybe there *are* aliens," I said. "Who knows?"

She slammed the door in my face, intentionally or not, and I watched her pull out and drive away. Her headlights swept across sword ferns coated with dust from the gravel road.

Oh, well, I thought.

I didn't go back to the Amazing Inn right away. Instead, I drifted over to the start of the dirt road to Amazing. But night was falling fast, and I still couldn't see any farther into the shadows. I wanted to walk down it a bit, to see if there was anything *to* see, but I hadn't brought a flashlight. Besides, I didn't want to leave Kevin to do the unpacking alone.

I carried another load of supplies into the house, and found Kevin in the hallway peering into one of the bedrooms.

"What are you doing?" I asked.

"Trying to decide who should get which room," he said. "I don't want anyone upset with us. I mean, come on, we have some pretty quirky friends."

I nodded toward the kitchen. "Come on, help me unpack."

"But—"

"It'll be fine."

He hesitated for a second, then he laughed. "Yeah, I'm being stupid."

Out in the front room, we both sort of stopped and looked around, taking in the awesomeness of the house, and the fact that we'd been able to rent something so cool. I was twenty-five years old, and I'd long ago stopped thinking of myself as a kid, but I didn't really think of myself as an adult either. Seeing this great house, knowing we'd somehow managed to get it for our wedding, was making me feel more grown up than a checking account or a credit card ever had.

"It's really happening," I said, feeling a little dizzy. "We're really doing this."

"I know," he said. "Can you believe it?"

By the way, I don't think I described Kevin. Basically, he was Zac Efron hot, with dark hair and a cute, impish grin. He was clean-cut and sensitive, and he wore contacts, and sometimes black-rimmed glasses, which I always said made him look like a hot TV nerd. None of this was the reason I was marrying him, but let's face it, it sure didn't hurt.

Kevin stepped up in front of me—he was a little taller than I was. I put down the groceries I was carrying, and he took me in his arms. He bent his head down, nuzzling his face in my neck.

"Mmmm," he said, "you smell like Russel."

"You smell like Kevin," I said, and he really did: clean and masculine.

"I love you."

"I love you too."

Then we kissed, and I thought to myself, *I am the luckiest person alive.* I definitely didn't feel dizzy anymore.

You're skeptical, aren't you? You're thinking back over all the things I mentioned in this chapter—my reluctance to mention the wedding at first, the little moments of tension between Kevin and me, our disagreement over having kids—and you're thinking, "Something's going on. There's something he isn't saying."

You might also be thinking: "There *has* to be something going on, because Russel is a neurotic nutbag who always over-thinks things. And now here he is doing the whole 'doth protest too much' thing, saying the opposite of what he really means."

That's it, isn't it? You think I'm being an unreliable narrator. You know, when it turns out the person telling a story is lying? Sometimes they're not even *aware* they're lying.

Well, you're wrong. There's nothing I'm not saying, and for the first time in my life, I wasn't being neurotic. The fact that the chapter opened with a dead end doesn't mean anything either. It wasn't a metaphor—it wasn't even a dead end. Remember? It turned out to be the parking lot of the place that was exactly where we were supposed to be.

This *wedding* was exactly where I was supposed to be. I really did love Kevin with all my heart, and I had absolutely no doubts or hesitations about marrying him. Kevin was a little anxious, true, but I knew he didn't have any doubts about marrying me either.

Of course now you might thinking: "If they don't have second thoughts about getting married, why is this a story? Why should I keep reading?" I told you earlier that I've been trying to make it as a screenwriter, and I know all too well that a good story requires conflict and drama. No conflict means no story. A happy, uneventful wedding is a *boring* wedding, except maybe to the people involved.

Okay, this is a better point. Honestly, you should have started with this point and not accused me of being neurotic.

But this is a different kind of story. Oh, plenty happens—you don't have to worry about that. But it's also a story where the main character isn't conflicted (and *isn't* neurotic).

Or maybe I *am* lying. If I really am a neurotic unreliable narrator, you can't believe anything I say.

I guess you'll have to keep reading to find out.

CHAPTER TWO

A half hour or so later, the doorbell rang, and I went to answer it.

Speaking of friends with quirks, the first of our guests to arrive were Gunnar and Min, two people who had known Kevin and me since high school. Min was with her new girlfriend, Ruby, who I'd never met before.

"You're here!" I said to the three of them. "Come in, come in!"

They all entered, eyeing the house, impressed. We didn't hug, because none of us were huggers (which I appreciated).

Gunnar was the kind of guy who sort of blended into the background, at least at first. He didn't give a lot of thought to the way he looked or dressed. For example, he was the only person I knew who combed his hair with an actual pocket comb.

But that was only the way he *looked*. When it came to who he actually was, he was the least average person I knew. There are people who operate on their own wavelength, and then there are people like Gunnar, who reject the radio spectrum entirely. A couple of years earlier, he'd even invented an iPhone app that had made him rich.

As he walked inside with his bags, Gunnar was grinning from ear to ear, totally excited. "Did you know that this place doesn't have gutters?" he said.

"What?" I said, confused.

"Outside! It has a rain dispersal system."

This didn't make me any less confused. "A what?"

"It's a way to get the water off a roof without using channels and spouts. The rain runs down into these panels which then sort of flings it out over the yard as droplets."

This was exactly the kind of thing I was talking about. This cool house with that amazing view, and Gunnar notices the gutters?

"I can't wait to see how it works in the rain!" Gunnar said.

"Well, we're sort of hoping it doesn't rain this week-end," I said, a little pointedly, "because it's, like, our wedding?"

"Oh, yeah, right," Gunnar said, but he still looked totally excited.

As he talked, I thought: *Don't tell Gunnar anything about Amazing, Washington.* I could see him becoming completely obsessed with the mystery of where every-one went.

"It's perfect," Min was saying, and she really did mean the house. "And that is an *incredible* view."

Min was sort of the opposite of Gunnar. She was this small Asian woman who made a huge impression, right from the beginning. She reminded me of one of those photos you see of a raccoon taking on a grizzly bear. She was incredibly smart, but more than anything, she had this air of authority about her. That was part of the reason why Kevin and I had chosen her to be the officiant at our wedding on Sunday—that and the fact that she was one of our closest friends. She'd registered online and everything, and Kevin and I already had the marriage certificate, so all we needed was for Min to sign it. We didn't even need to have an actual ceremony if we didn't want to, although that would have left us with some pretty annoyed guests on Sunday.

"Thanks," I said to Min. "So how *are* you?"

"Freaking out about the election, for one thing. Are people crazy or just stupid? After all this time, is it really possible that they don't understand what's at stake?"

"I've already told her," Ruby said to me, "no politics this weekend."

I smiled. "It's fine. She's among freaked-out friends."

"Oh!" Min said. "Ruby, this is Russel. And Kevin! I keep forgetting you guys haven't actually met yet."

"Nice to meet you, Ruby," Kevin said from the other side of the room. "Hi, Min. Hi, Gunnar."

"Hi," I said to Ruby, shaking her hand.

It's probably sexist to describe a woman as looking like an Amazonian warrior, but that's what I thought seeing Ruby. It wasn't only that she was tall and athletic (but she was), or that she had dark skin (Latina?), or that she had a no-nonsense haircut and wasn't wearing makeup. It was that there was a fearlessness about her, like she was unconquerable, with also maybe the tiniest touch of crazy in her eyes.

This made me smile. When it came to who Min was dating, I never knew what to expect.

I was getting Gunnar, Min, and Ruby settled into their rooms when the doorbell rang again, and it occurred to me that this must be part of living on an island:

23

things happen in waves, because of the coming and going of the ferries.

"Nate!" I heard Kevin say. This was one of Kevin's best friends, his roommate from college. I'd never met him before either.

"Well," Nate said, "ain't this a ripper of a place?"

There was something about his voice that made me stop in the hallway. I knew Nate was Australian (which is why I'd never met him—after graduation, he'd gone back to Melbourne for med school), and he definitely had an accent. But he sounded sexy too, confident and cocky.

Curious, I edged my way down the hallway to the main room.

I saw Nate before he saw me.

The voice was no lie. He had dirty blond hair, great posture, and the perfect amount of tan. He was also a little rough around the edges, rumpled in all the right places. There was a carefree, outdoors-y quality about him, like one of those guys you see climbing rock cliffs in car commercials.

Nate's eyes found me lingering in the shadows, and his face broke into a grin.

"Hey, now, there he is," he said. "You must be the ol' ball and chain!"

I immediately bristled. I'd always hated that expression—"ball and chain."

But this was Kevin's best friend, so I plastered a smile onto my face and stepped forward.

"Hey, there, Nate," I said. "It's nice to finally meet you."

"Likewise! And don't worry, mate, now that I'm here, we won't be having no run-away groom." At that, he grabbed Kevin with one hand on his arm and another around the back of his neck, pretending like he was going to take him down.

And in a flash, I realized that maybe Nate wasn't as handsome as I'd thought.

This had happened to me before—meeting someone, thinking they're hot, and then getting to know them (and not liking them), and thinking, "How could I ever have thought this person was hot in the first place?" But it had never happened this fast.

Kevin laughed and said, "I don't think you need to worry."

"Oh, yeah," Nate said. "I heard all the stories!" Then he winked at Kevin, and Kevin blushed and chuckled, and Nate laughed outright.

I wasn't even going to *try* to parse all that.

Min and Ruby stepped into view, with Gunnar behind them, and we made introductions all around.

Then Kevin said to Nate, "Let me show you your room."

I was determined to not let my annoyance with Nate color the weekend, so I added, "Yeah, and then we have something very important to do before dinner."

Everyone looked at me like I was being completely serious.

"*Cocktails!* What did you *think* I meant?" I said, and everyone laughed.

After the new arrivals had unpacked, we all gathered for drinks and chips around the kitchen island. The wedding on Sunday was being catered, but Kevin and I had stopped at the grocery store earlier that day to get food for the rest of the weekend. So now we assembled a salad and got the take-and-bake pizzas ready while we waited for the next ferry, which wasn't due for another half-hour.

"So what's new," I said to Min and Gunnar. "Tell me everything."

"Nothing much," Min said.

"Oh, come *on*," Gunnar said, busting he was so excited. "Tell 'em about your new job!"

"What new job?" I asked.

"She's working for Elon Musk!" Gunnar said. Elon Musk was the guy who created PayPal and Tesla. Needless to say, he was now amazingly rich.

I looked at Min. "Really?" I said. "Why didn't you tell me?"

"Because it's nothing," she said. "It's no big deal."

"It's a *huge* deal!" Gunnar said. "It's the most expensive, privately-financed space exploration project in human history!"

"*Space* exploration?" I said.

Min shrugged it off. "Oh, they're making noises about a mission to Mars by 2030—a private-public partnership. But it's just public relations. It probably won't happen."

"A *manned* mission to Mars!" Gunnar said.

"Wait," I said to Min. "Mars? By *2030*? What are you doing?"

"She's designing the ship," Ruby said.

"*What?*" I said. Now it was my head that was almost exploding, but none of this surprised me in the least. I've already said how brilliant Min was.

"I'm *helping* to design *part* of the ship," Min said.

"A ship to *Mars*!" I said. "That's so cool!"

"It really is," Kevin said, nodding.

Min let herself grin at last, in an adorably sheepish way. "It kind of is, isn't it?" She looked at me. "But tell me what's going on with you."

"Nothing's going on with me," I said. "My life is incredibly boring right now."

"Except for the fact that you're getting married Sunday," Min said.

My face burned red. Kevin glared at me too.

"Oh, yeah," I said, trying to laugh it off. "Except for *that*. But seriously, tell us about this mission to Mars."

So she did, and it was exactly as interesting as you'd think.

At one point while Min was talking, I turned around and saw that Gunnar was doing something with the broccoli for the salad. He wasn't chopping it, which was what I'd asked him to do. No, he had taken the stalks and stuck them into glasses filled with blue liquid.

"Uh, what is this?" I asked.

"I'm trying to turn the broccoli blue," he said, as if it was the most obvious thing in the world.

I stared at him.

"I found some food coloring in the cabinet," he went on. "I'm seeing if you can do the same thing with broccoli that you can do with celery. You know, how the plant draws the color up into its leaves?"

This was so typically Gunnar. Min may have been planning a trip to Mars, but Gunnar was already living on his own little planet. Back when I'd been living with him and Min, this might have annoyed me a little, but now I felt nothing but affection for them both.

"I've missed you guys so much!" I said.

"I know," Min said. "We've missed you too. Why in the world did you and Kevin have to move to Los Angeles?"

"It's working!" Gunnar said, meaning the broccoli. "No, wait, that's just the reflection off the bag of chips."

"Hey," Nate said, "did you guys know there are stairs down to the beach?"

Nate was standing over in the doorway out to the deck. To be honest, I'd been sort of glad when he'd wandered away from the conversation. But I guess I had sort of been leaving both him and Ruby out, and that made me feel guilty.

Ruby immediately perked up. "Really?"

"Yeah," Nate said. "You wanna check it out?"

"You kidding? I'm so there!"

"But first," Nate said, approaching the kitchen and grabbing a beer, "one for the road."

As he turned away, he flipped the bottle in the air—casually, but pretty darn expertly.

"Oh!" Ruby said. "Like Tom Cruise in *Cocktail*!"

He did it again, and it was all very impressive, not to mention light-hearted and carefree, but of course the only thing I could think of was "damage deposit."

Soon they thundered off to explore the beach.

The rest of us were silent after that. I felt a little less guilty about leaving Nate and Ruby out of the conversation after the deal with the beer bottle. But I didn't want Min to know that.

"Ruby seems great," I said to Min.

Min smiled and dipped a chip in some guacamole.

"It's funny though," I went on, "and please don't take this the wrong way, because I love you like Life-savers, but she seems a little different from you."

Right on cue, Ruby and Nate shrieked somewhere out on the steps down to the beach—a fun shriek, not like they were falling off a cliff.

"If by 'different,'" Min said, "you mean 'pretty much my complete opposite in every way,' you're right. She's either going to be the love of my life, or I'm making the biggest *mistake* of my life. Either way, it should be interesting."

The four of us sipped and crunched.

"Nate seems great too," Min said, and Gunnar nodded, but I didn't.

"He's a really good guy," Kevin said. He bent down to search for something in the lower kitchen shelves. "I met him my freshman year, but we didn't become roommates until later. He's sort of an 'in the moment' guy, which is why it's so funny he went on to become a doctor. But he was the perfect college friend." He rattled the pots, frustrated. "*Really?* The money we're spending and there aren't any pizza pans?"

"What about cookie sheets?" I said, pointing.

"They're not big enough," he said.

"It's okay, we'll make 'em fit." Honestly, I was a little annoyed Kevin was being so pissy about the pans, especially in front of our friends. I guess he was feeling stressed.

Gunnar lifted his glass. "I want to make a toast," he said. "To Kevin and Russ."

"What?" I said, surprised. Gunnar was the kind of guy who tried to turn broccoli blue, not the kind of guy who made wedding toasts.

"Russ," he said, "you may not remember this, but I was there the first time you met Kevin."

"You were *not*," I said. Gunnar was strange, but he wasn't so strange that he'd be lurking in the bushes spying on two guys in a park in the middle of the night. Was he?

"You couldn't have been there," Kevin said. "Russel and I were alone."

"What?" Gunnar said. "No, the whole class was there."

Everyone looked at him blankly.

"It was the seventh grade," Gunnar said. "In middle school? Kevin transferred in from another district."

I let myself relax. Gunnar was right. That was the first day I'd ever seen Kevin, even if I didn't actually talk to him until weeks, or maybe even years, later.

Kevin smiled, relaxing at last. "I remember that. I was so nervous."

"I don't believe it," I said. "You didn't look nervous at all."

Gunnar nodded, basically agreeing with me. "The teacher asked you to tell the class something about yourself, and you said, 'My name is Kevin Land, and I'm going to be an astronaut.'"

Kevin blushed. "I did *not*! Oh, God, that sounds like such a little kid thing to say. And I *was* nervous. I was terrified."

"It didn't seem that way," Gunnar said. "You totally sold it."

"It's not too late," I said to Kevin. "Maybe Min can get you on the first ship to Mars."

"I'm serious," she said. "It's not going to happen."

"I remember now," Kevin said. "I had just done this camp thing at Cape Canaveral."

"And did you see sparks?" Min asked Gunnar. "Did you know Russel and Kevin were destined to be to-gether?"

"You didn't even know I was gay back then," I said to Gunnar. "Or did you?"

"I knew you were different. That's why I liked you."

This made me smile. I'd liked Gunnar the first time I met him, in the fourth grade, for exactly the same reason. I'd tried hard to hide my weirdness from my classmates, and Gunnar had too, but it never worked: he was *too* different.

"What did you think?" Min asked me, meaning about Kevin.

I had to think back. When it came to Kevin, there was a lot in my brain to untangle. But I did have a vague memory of the whole encounter.

"I knew he'd be the most popular boy in class," I said. "Which he was."

"I was *not*," Kevin said, wrestling with the plastic wrap on one of the take-and-bake pizzas.

I didn't dignify his denial with a response. "I think the whole class knew, just from the way he looked, the way he stood," I said. "Even Jim Madsen, the most popular guy in class until then. I think he took one look at Kevin and said, 'Well, that's it, I'm done.'"

Kevin kept blushing.

"Did you think he was hot?" Gunnar asked.

"Probably," I said. "Everyone thought he was hot."

Kevin glanced at me. "I remember what I thought of you."

"You do *not*. I'm sure you didn't even notice me."

"Are you kidding? That hair? I noticed you right away. And I thought you were adorable."

(I have red hair—more auburn, really.)

Now I blushed.

"We've gone over all this before," Kevin said. "Why do you think I teased you?"

This made me smile. In high school, Kevin had sometimes stolen my underwear in the locker room and thrown it around to the other jocks. If anyone had tried to tell me then that he'd been doing it because he had a crush on me, because he was trying to get close to me, it would have blown my mind.

"I wonder if our eyes met," I said.

"What?" Kevin asked.

"That first day. You say you noticed me, and I know I noticed you. I wonder what we looked like together. Wouldn't you kill to go back in time and see?"

Kevin's face softened, and he had sort of a dreamy smile. "Yeah." Remember when I said he seemed sort of pissy? That was long gone by now.

Meanwhile, the picture in my mind of Kevin back in the seventh grade was becoming clearer and clearer. He was wearing a blue shirt and jeans. He'd recently gotten a haircut—or maybe he always kept his hair that neatly trimmed. Yes, I thought he was hot.

And now I've ended up with him, I said to myself.

Gunnar lifted his glass again. "To Russ and Kevin," he said, "and to destiny!"

Who in the world wouldn't drink to that?

But once we'd finished toasting, Kevin turned his attention back to the pizza—which unfortunately, really was too big for the cookie sheet.

"God *damn* it!" he said, frustrated again, and that's when I took over and made the executive call to cook the pizzas directly on the oven rack.

CHAPTER THREE

Forty or so minutes later, the doorbell rang again, which meant that the next ferry must have finally arrived on the island. I answered the door.

"Vernie!" I said, grinning like a kid getting a triple-scoop ice cream cone.

It was my friend Vernie Rose, a seventy-four year old woman, carrying an overnight bag. Vernie was even shorter than Min, but wider at the hips, with silver hair that was cut in sort of a bowl. She wore diamond cat-rim glasses, but it was her eyes that were doing most of the sparkling.

Vernie was a retired screenwriter—she had once even been nominated for an Oscar (for a short film she wrote). We'd met a few years earlier, and now she was my screenwriting mentor. When it came time for Kevin and me to figure out who we wanted to spend the whole wedding weekend with us, I knew right away I wanted Vernie.

She stepped inside, looking around the house. "Nice place," she said. "Where's the booze?"

I laughed. "How was the ferry ride?"

"Horrible. I'm too old for this shit. But I'm pleased as punch to be here. But first I need to spend a penny."

I knew that meant she needed to use the bathroom, so I pointed out the way.

When she got back, she said, "You thought I was kidding about the booze, didn't you?"

But I'd totally known that was coming, so I pulled a glass of wine out from behind my back.

"Oh, you're gooood!" she said, taking the glass. "I knew there was a reason I liked you."

Right then, the doorbell rang one last time, and I opened it.

"Otto!" I said.

"Russel!" he said, and we actually did hug.

I'd met Otto years ago when were both sixteen and counselors at a summer camp. We'd even dated for a few months after that, but that was all long over. Now he was an actor living in Los Angeles, which was where I'd reconnected with him the year before. But Otto was a burn survivor. When he was seven years old, he got into some gasoline and matches, and now he had a big burn on his shoulder and one-half of his face. Over the years, he'd had some corrective surgery. Plus, he was a pretty good-looking guy to begin with, even more so now that he'd grown into his looks.

Still, for a long time, he'd struggled, because it was hard enough being an unknown actor even without big scars on your face. But earlier that year, he'd landed a role on a network sitcom called *Hammered*, about this guy, Mike Hammer, and his friends living in a college dorm. Otto played Dustin, one of Mike's dorm-mates, who also happened to have scars on his face.

Truthfully, except for Otto, the show wasn't that special. I mean, it was mostly about guys trying to get laid, and dealt with issues like "the friend zone," and fuck buddies, and how for some Millennials, porn is supposedly better than real sex—comedy themes that were completely tapped out five years ago.

Still, it was incredible watching someone I knew on television. Better still, when the show had debuted in early June, Dustin had quickly become the break-out character. It's not every day that someone with scars on their face gets cast in a sitcom. It was a little like Laverne Cox on *Orange is the New Black* being the first transgender actress playing a transgender character on an actual TV program.

The one problem with all this was that ever since Otto had become famous, I hadn't seen very much of him. I didn't hold it against him—I could only imagine how busy he was. But we'd gotten pretty close before that, and I missed him.

"Otto Digmore!" Vernie said before I could even introduce them (they'd never met either).

"Vernie Rose," Otto said.

"I've heard so much about you," they both said to each other at exactly the same time.

"Otto!" said Min, behind us.

"Min!" Otto said. Gunnar stepped into view too. "*Gunnar!*"

The three of them ran together and hugged like one of them had been shipwrecked on an island for six years—even Min who, like me, was not a hugger. Min and Gunnar had known Otto at summer camp too, and the three of them hadn't seen each other since way back then.

"You look so different," Gunnar said.

"Fantastic," Min said. "You look *fantastic*."

The weird part was, Otto looked different even since I'd last seen him. Was it the fact that he was famous now, that I'd watched him on TV? Honestly, it seemed like more than that. And it wasn't just the obviously expensive clothes and the new, incredibly flattering haircut. He had a confidence he'd never had before. He and I used to joke that the secret to success in Holly-wood was to simply *act* successful, but now I saw that actual success looked different than fake success. It wasn't as eager-to-please. Anyway, it flattered him too.

"God, how long has it been?" Otto said to Min and Gunnar. "Ten years? We were all such kids."

As they talked, I introduced Vernie to Nate and Ruby, who were back from the beach.

At one point, I overheard Gunnar saying to Otto, "It's so great, you're being famous and everything."

Otto shook his head and even blushed a little, perfectly endearing. "I'm not famous," he said.

"You *so* are!" I called. "And you totally, *totally* de-serve it."

At that point, he just smiled modestly, but right after that, he peeled off from the others to go wash his hands before dinner.

A few minutes later, we gathered everyone at the dinner table. Kevin and I stood together at one end.

"We'd like to say a couple of things," Kevin said. "First, just so you know, we've installed hidden cameras throughout the house, including the bathrooms. So if any of you do anything questionable, the two of us will definitely know."

People laughed, but Gunnar said, "Really?" and when I told him no, he actually looked kind of disappointed.

"No, seriously," Kevin said, "Russel and I really want to thank you all for coming. It means a lot to us. But we also wanted to explain why we hadn't asked any of you to be our best man. Or best woman."

"Best person," Min said, and I pointed at her.

"Why?" Nate said, mock-indignant.

"Because we hate you all," Kevin said.

Nate snorted, and everyone else laughed again. Kevin was killing this little speech of his, which made me happy for a lot of reasons, but especially because it meant he'd finally relaxed about the weekend.

"Actually," I said, "it's because we didn't want to have to choose. The way we see it, you're *all* our best persons." My eyes found Ruby and Nate. "Well, except for you guys, because I only just met you. But I'm sure if I *knew* you, I would absolutely want you as a 'best person' too."

Yes, this was mostly me being diplomatic (I couldn't imagine ever liking Nate that much).

Ruby hoisted her drink. "I'm right there with ya!" she said.

Kevin took my hand, and we faced the gathering again. "Anyway," he said, "that's what we wanted to say. That we love you all, and we're really happy you could be here with us."

Everyone hooted and applauded, and told us they loved us too, and how happy they were to be there. After that, we ate and talked, but I couldn't help thinking about what Kevin had said. The stuff about not wanting to pick a "best person"? It was the actual truth, something he and I had decided beforehand.

But as I looked around the table, I wondered: If someone put a gun to my head, who would I pick—not only as my best person, but as my best friend? The whole idea of a best friend was really kind of stupid—something from grade school, like wanting to be an astronaut when you grew up. But I still wondered who it would be. Min? She was definitely the person I confided in the most, even now that I lived in Los Angeles, and I think she probably understood me better than anyone. But Gunnar was the kind of guy you could count on for absolutely anything, no questions asked, and Min and I joked a lot about how he understood more than he sometimes let on. Otto and I had once been boyfriends, which gave you a special kind of intimacy (you'll note that he was the only person I hugged at the front door). Now that we lived in the same city, he and I had ended up becoming really close—at least before his career had taken off. And there was Vernie, the person who had helped me find meaning in my life by getting me to realize I wanted to be a screenwriter, and who was now the world's greatest mentor.

Then there was Kevin, the guy I was marrying. The instant I thought of it, I realized that *he* was my best friend, no matter how you sliced it.

The best man is also the groom, I thought. Who knew?

All of which made me realize (again) what a lucky guy I was, and that I'd pretty much have to have blue broccoli for brains to complain about anything in my life.

After dinner, we all cleaned up, and Vernie helped me load the dishwater.

"So what's new in Hollywood?" she asked me.

"Well, *A Cup of Joe* is officially dead," I said. *A Cup of Joe* was an indie movie project I'd written that some friends and I had been trying to set up in Los Angeles. We'd come really close to getting financing a couple of times, but it had always fallen through. In the end, everyone had given up and moved on to other projects.

"Just dead or truly dead?"

Everyone in Hollywood knows that nothing is ever really dead—that there's always one more place to try, one more hustle to play, or maybe an unexpected change in the marketplace. But it's somehow also true that sometimes a project finally seems truly dead, and you have to learn to let it go.

"Truly dead, I think," I said.

"Well, I'm really sorry to hear that. It was a damn good script. But they're all spins at the roulette wheel. You know that, right? There's a *huge* element of luck in all of this, just flat-out random chance. That's why you can't get bogged down with any one project. You need to have at least five scripts always ready to go. Do you have five scripts ready to go?"

"Ma'am, yes, *ma'am*!" I said, saluting like a soldier.

Vernie laughed.

"I've decided I need a new strategy," I said.

"I'm intrigued. Go on."

"Well, with *A Cup of Joe*, it all boiled down to money. Everyone wants to make a feature film, but no one has any money. So I've decided to write a single-location script. Something completely bare-bones that can be produced for a hundred thousand dollars or less."

Single-location scripts were suddenly all the rage among aspiring screenwriters in Hollywood. The idea was that the whole story is set in a single location (or two), so the movie can be filmed fast and inexpensively.

Vernie thought about it, then nodded. "I guess that makes sense."

"You know," I said, "movies like *Buried*, or *Devil*, or *Moon*, or *Wrecked*, or *ATM*, or *Locke*? All those writers got lots of attention for good scripts that could be filmed really cheap."

"*Twelve Angry Men*," Vernie said.

"Yeah!"

"What are they about?"

"Well," I said, "*Buried* is about someone trapped in a coffin. *Moon* is about someone trapped in a moon station, *Devil* is about people trapped in an elevator, *Wrecked* is about someone trapped in the wreckage of a car, *ATM* is—"

"Okay, okay, I get the idea. Do they have to have one-word titles?"

"No, that's just a coincidence."

"There's just one problem," Vernie said.

"What's that?"

"Movies are an inherently visual medium. And also a medium that depends on movement."

"What's your point? That no one wants to see a movie set in a single location?"

"You said it."

"But the writers are using their self-imposed limitations to explore a particular theme," I said. "These are movies that are literally *about* being trapped, so the setting reinforces the theme. Besides, the critics love 'em."

"Oh, the *critics*." She made a motion like she was jacking off, and I laughed.

"Well," I said, "in addition to having one-word titles and being about people who are trapped, you know what else those movies all have in common?"

"What's that?"

"They actually got *made*. Unlike, oh, I don't know, the twelve screenplays *I've* written?"

Vernie smiled. "Good point. But do me a favor?"

"Sure."

"Never forget the whole point of movies."

"What's that?" I asked.

"Movie moments."

I stared at her.

"You know, movie moments?" she went on. "Those moments in every good movie where everything comes perfectly together—the writing, the acting, the visuals—with some great emotional punch? Like when Brody sees the shark for the first time in *Jaws* and says, 'You're gonna need a bigger boat.' Or in *Spartacus* when Kirk Douglas stands up and says, 'I am Spartacus!' And then the rest of the crowd stands up too, one by one, all saying that they're Spartacus too."

"The cockroach scene in *Snowpiercer*," I said.

"I don't know what that is," Vernie said, "but I'm sure you're right. A movie moment is any moment in a movie where it all comes together—it's larger than life, but also somehow perfectly *about* life. They're actually the reason we go to the movies in the first place, because they perfectly capture some emotion that we've all felt, and clarify exactly what the movie is trying to say."

I kept staring at her, but now I looked annoyed.

"Now what?" she said.

"You've been my mentor for how long now? Two years? And you're only telling me about movie moments *now*?"

"Well, it's kind of implied in everything I told you before."

"Yes, but I didn't know there was an actual technical *term*."

"A term I basically just made up."

"That's completely beside the point!" I said. I kept scowling, determined to make her squirm. Alas, Vernie rarely squirms.

"Let's move on," she said. "What ideas do you have so far for a single-location script?"

Reluctantly, I withdrew my scowl.

"Well," I said, "my first idea was a script called *Couch Potatoes*. It's about four guys who are roommates."

"Why are they all guys?" Vernie asked.

"Good point. Okay, three guys and a girl."

"That's almost worse. The whole Smurfette Principle."

I smiled, impressed that Vernie knew about the Smurfette Principle (which is the story trope where there is only one major female character, usually a completely stereotypical one, among a large cast of diverse males, like in *The Fantastic Four*, *Guardians of the Galaxy*, *The Avengers*, *The Teenage Mutant Ninja Turtles*, *Now You See Me*, *Harry Potter*, *Fast & Furious*, *Winnie the Pooh*, *The Smurfs*, and, oh, a zillion other things).

"Okay, it's four *guys*," I said, and Vernie nodded. "And they're jerky to the woman who lives next door. But she turns out to be a gypsy, and she curses them so they can't get up off the couch until they somehow solve the gypsy's curse."

She stared at me without saying a word.

"It's not *that* bad," I said. "Is it?"

"Apart from the romaphobia?"

Nate interrupted us, so I didn't get a chance to ask what romaphobia was.

"Screw the gas fire pit—Ruby and I built a bonfire down on the beach," he said. "You guys wanna join us?"

I felt a little judged by Nate, that he had to build a "real" fire. Even so, I looked at Vernie. "Shall we?"

"Oh, I don't think so," she said.

"Really? Why not?"

"Because I saw that stairway down to the beach. I'd never make it at night."

"Sure, you will. I'll help you."

"No, you and your friends go, and I think I'll turn in early."

The rest of us did go down to the fire on the beach, and we all smoked a little weed (which, for the record, is perfectly legal in Washington State).

But Kevin and I had flown up from California on Wednesday, and we'd had a zillion things to do to get ready for the weekend, and now we were both exhausted. So we retired early too, right after midnight.

When we got to the master bedroom, Kevin disappeared into the bathroom to get ready for bed. I stopped, looking around the room.

Something didn't feel right. I couldn't figure out what it was.

It was definitely an incredible bedroom. It had a high ceiling, a king-sized bed, and a separate seating area next to a gigantic window facing the water. I'd slept in nice bedrooms before, but only when my parents were paying, never with Kevin. Was that what felt weird—the fact that Kevin and I had never slept together in a room this nice? We'd been living together for more than a year, and sleeping together for longer than that, but it had always been on futons in cheap apartments or tiny bedrooms, not massive bedrooms with en-suite bathrooms and Jacuzzi tubs.

"This place is really something," I said, even though I wasn't sure Kevin could hear me in the bathroom with the door closed.

I stepped up to the window to look outside, but it was dark now, so I was mostly looking into a big black void.

"What?" Kevin said behind me.

I turned and suddenly my view got a whole lot better: he was standing there in a tight t-shirt and boxer briefs.

"Nothing," I said.

"How do you think it's going?" he said, flossing his teeth.

"The weekend? It seems like it's going great. Great speech, by the way. Oh, hey, isn't it fun the way Nate and Ruby are hitting it off?"

"Yeah," Kevin said, distracted.

"But I've heard that before, how a lot of straight guys and lesbians really click. I think I even read how their brains are a lot alike or something. Like straight women and gay guys, except straight guy/lesbian relationships aren't a media stereotype, so you never hear about 'em."

"Hmm."

Kevin wandered back into the bathroom to brush his teeth. That's when I realized what was wrong with the room.

"The room has no blinds or curtains," I said.

"What?" Kevin said from the bathroom.

"Nothing," I said, but I couldn't help but think it was going to be hard to stay sleeping once the sun came up the next morning.

He joined me in the main room and started searching through his overnight bag.

"*Damn* it," he said.

"What?" I said.

"I forgot my charge cord at my parents' house."

"It's okay, we can share mine."

"Fuck, fuck, fuck!"

I didn't say anything for a second. Then I said, "What's wrong?"

"I just told you!" Kevin said.

"I mean in general. It seems like something's been going on with you today. It's not about our getting married, is it?"

Kevin froze for a second. Then he sighed and sank down onto the bed. He looked like one of those abandoned barns about to collapse.

"No," he said. "Well, yes, but it's not about *getting* married. I just want everything to go well. I mean, it's our *wedding*. The whole point of a wedding is for two people to stand up in front of their friends and family, and tell everyone how much the two people love each other, how important they are to each other. That's how people know to take them seriously as a couple, that they *are* a couple."

I nodded vaguely. Everything Kevin said made sense.

"But if everything is all messed up," Kevin said, "what's the point in doing it?"

"What makes you think things'll be messed up?" I asked.

"I just checked the weather. It's supposed to rain this weekend. And, I mean, a *lot*."

"Kevin!" We'd agreed we weren't going to check the weather forecast since (a) there wasn't anything we could do about it, (b) we had a back-up plan where we moved everyone inside if it rained. Kevin and I disagreed on weather forecasts anyway: I'd always thought they were mostly bullshit, more like silly horoscopes than actual science.

"I know, I know," Kevin said.

"I'm sure everything'll work out fine." When he didn't answer, I added, "Do you want a blowjob? Help you relax?"

(Incidentally, did other couples talk like this? I sort of doubted that very many straight couples did, but I figured other gay couples might. Then again, I'd never really been part of any other gay couples, not long-term anyway, so I didn't know.)

"Thanks," he said, "but I'm too tired."

I nodded, then I headed into the bathroom to do my own thing. After that, I turned out the light and climbed into the bed next to Kevin.

The mattress was so big that it took me a moment to find him.

"Hellooooo?" I said, making an echo with my voice, pawing through the covers. "Is there anyone *in* here?" Finally, I found him, lean and tight in his soft cotton undies.

I cuddled up next to him. "It's going to be okay," I said. "I mean it. This is going to be the best wedding of all time."

He didn't answer.

I put my hand on his forehand. "Nod if you hear me."

He laughed and nodded.

Then, of course, I slipped my hand down into his boxer-briefs and found that he was rock-hard.

"I thought you said you were exhausted," I said.

"That was almost three minutes ago."

I laughed and started kissing him.

And just for the record? I still wasn't feeling any weirdness about the wedding, getting cold feet or anything.

In fact, if anyone was being a little neurotic, it was Kevin. How nice was that for a change?

CHAPTER FOUR

Sure enough, the sun shining in the windows woke me up early the next morning.

What's the deal with curtain-less bedrooms anyway? Over the years, I'd ended up in more of them than you'd think, or bedrooms with these totally worthless, gossamer-y curtains that didn't stop any light at all. This always seemed vaguely hostile to me, like the morning person who decorated the bedroom was making a little moral judgment on the idea of someone actually sleeping in. Or maybe they couldn't even *conceive* of the idea that the whole world wasn't exactly like them, up at the crack of dawn.

But at least the sun *was* shining, which meant the weather forecast had been wrong about the weekend rain, so far anyway.

Beside me in bed, Kevin somehow slumbered blissfully on. I didn't want to wake him, so I quietly dressed and slipped out into the main house.

I was the only person up, and everything was so incredibly quiet. It wasn't like being back in Los Angeles with the never-ending sounds of the city: the whoosh of the freeways, the sound of the sirens.

I made a pot of coffee in the kitchen, then carried a cup out to the deck.

It was still cold out, and everything was wet with morning dew, but the view of the water was fantastic. I loved the way it filled the channel, perfectly hugging the bays, glistening like liquid eternity. The air smelled of pine with a salty mist from the water below me.

But as I sat there, I realized the island wasn't as quiet as I'd first thought. The trees all around the house creaked, squirrels skittered in the branches, and birds twittered. Down on the beach, waves lolled against the rocks (and I caught a whiff of the seaweed that had probably washed up on them).

I suddenly remembered what Christie had told me the day before about the abandoned town of Amazing, Washington.

I hadn't finished my coffee yet, but I went back into the house. I was still the only one up, so I found my jacket and shoes, and headed off across the yard, through the parking lot, to the start of that little road that led to Amazing.

The second I stepped onto the road, something seemed different, but I couldn't quite figure out what it was. The road wasn't well-used: it was just two dirt tire tracks winding through the pine trees.

I found myself growing weirdly excited. What would I find at the end? Christie had said there were ruins, but what did that mean exactly? The road was mostly covered with a scattering of leaves and pine needles, everything wet from the dampness of autumn, so the ground felt soft, and I couldn't hear my own footsteps. The forest was oddly quiet too. I didn't hear any birds or squirrels now, and the trees weren't creaking like they had been out on the deck at the house either. It felt like the forest was holding its breath in anticipation of what was going to happen next.

I picked up my pace, eager to get to the end of the road.

It turned to the right, around a bend, and then made another turn, to the left, down a hill toward the water. Now I held *my* breath.

I found myself facing another hill—or, rather, a rocky promontory that looked out over the water. It was rough and jagged, but still covered with trees and ferns. To the right, a flat apron of land looped around a little rocky cove. The trees and undergrowth were still thick—so thick I could barely make out the beach.

But as for the road itself, it just ended. It wasn't even a cul-de-sac. It was a slightly wider area where a car could park or turn around.

I didn't see the ruins Christie had mentioned, or any sign of the town of Amazing at all. There was only the forest.

Around me, the trees were creaking again, and waves washed against the beach. Seagulls screeched, fighting over something in the rocks.

Well, that was anticlimactic, I thought. As usual, I'd let my imagination get away from me. As for Amazing, Christie the Crackpot had probably made the whole thing up.

Still, I'd come this far, so I figured I should at least look around.

I came to the end of the road, then followed a narrow footpath down to the cove. At one point, someone had made a bunch of stacks of flat grey rocks—cairns, I guess they're called. Some of them poked up out of the sword ferns, and a few of them stuck out into the trail itself, so the path veered around them. There was something sort of otherworldly about them, and I felt a little like I was walking through the skeletal remains of a dinosaur. Somewhere to my right, a stream gurgled, but I couldn't see it through the undergrowth.

Suddenly there was someone right in front of me. I'd almost run right into them.

"Oh!" I said, pulling back.

"Russel?" the person said.

It was Min.

"Oh, my God, you scared me!" I said. She was wearing earth-tones (typical for her), so she'd blended right into the undergrowth. Plus, I'd been distracted by the stream.

"What are you doing up so early?" she asked me. She knew the hours I usually kept.

"No curtains in the master bedroom. What about you?"

"Ruby snores."

I felt bad for her, but was actually glad I'd run into her out here. As excited as I was to gather all my best friends together in one house, I'd been worried that I wouldn't be able to spend any time with them one-on-one. Min and I didn't live in the same city anymore, and I really missed her.

"Also..." she said.

"What?" I said.

"Well, there was this album back in the inn—this book of articles. It talked all about this little town of Amazing that the place is supposedly named after."

"I know! Isn't it cool? The manager told me about it yesterday. But she said the residents were abducted by aliens, so I figured she was making it up."

Min smiled sardonically.

"There were really articles, though, huh?" I said. "And did they say if the residents really all supposedly disappeared overnight?"

She nodded.

"So where is it?" I asked. "Christie said there were ruins, but I don't see any—"

And it was strange. All of a sudden I saw how this little cove, and the apron of flat land that surrounded it, was actually a pretty good place for at least a small town.

Min saw it too.

"There," Min said, pointing to the cairns I'd seen earlier.

Except that's not what they were. They were the remnants of stone foundations. The houses had long since fallen away, and at some point whatever they'd used for mortar in the foundations must have deteriorated too. So now even most of the foundations had collapsed, but a few small sections remained upright. If you connected the dots, you could see they formed rectangles—the outlines of what had once been buildings. I could make out at least three foundations, but there were probably more in the trees. There might even have been a "main street" at one point.

There were ruins here after all, really obvious ones. I'd just missed them.

It sort of gave me the chills knowing that Amazing was real. Maybe that meant the story about everyone disappearing was also real.

Where did they go? I wondered.

I wanted to ask Min, but I felt stupid. I had a way of letting my imagination get away from me. It's possible I could even be a teeny-tiny bit melodramatic, and Min had been known to (affectionately) tease me about it.

We started meandering among the ruins. Christie had said something about an abandoned well, but I didn't see that anywhere. That was all I needed, to accidentally fall down an abandoned well. On the other hand, it would definitely give this weekend some drama.

"So," Min asked me, "how are you feeling?"

"What?" I said.

"About the wedding."

"Fine. I mean, Kevin is stressed, but I'm great."

"Yeah, I sensed that. About Kevin."

"I wish I could do something," I said. "He's such a good guy. But for the time being, I'm trying to be supportive and just listen."

Min nodded.

"I liked what Gunnar said last night," I said. "About how Kevin and I first met. And how we're *destined* to be together."

"You so are."

I stopped at one of the stacks of rocks—part of a foundation. I touched it with my foot, and to my surprise, a couple of the rocks fell over with a clatter.

I laughed. "Isn't that funny? It's been standing all this time, and I barely touch it and it collapses."

Min smiled, but didn't laugh. I stopped laughing too. Suddenly it didn't seem so funny anymore. I tried to rebuild it, but I couldn't figure it out. It was a puzzle where nothing seemed to fit.

"You okay?" Min said, watching me.

"Huh? Yeah. Why?"

"It feels like there's something on your mind."

Min knew me really well, and at that moment in time, it was kind of annoying the shit out of me.

"No!" I said, but maybe it was more to myself than to her. "For the first time in my life, I'm determined to *not* be neurotic about something. *Kevin* is the neurotic one this time."

"What's going on?" she said.

I didn't answer.

"Oh, come on," she said. "You think I'm going to tell?"

She kept staring at me, her eyes never blinking, a little like a Russian interrogator.

I cracked under the pressure.

Okay, yes, there may have been one little thing that had been on my mind about the wedding. But it was such a teensy-tiny thing that I really wasn't lying before when I said I was perfectly calm about getting married. It doesn't mean I'm an unreliable narrator, and it *absolutely* didn't mean I was being neurotic.

"It really doesn't have anything to do with Kevin," I said. "I love him completely and totally, and I want to spend my whole life with him."

"Who wouldn't?"

"I also don't have cold feet, or last-minute jitters, or anything like that."

"Of course not."

"But, I mean, *marriage*. What does that even mean?"

"It means whatever you and Kevin want it to mean," Min said.

"Oh, everyone always says that, but what does that mean *really*?"

"It means a lot," she said. I started to talk, and she interrupted me. "No, wait, hear me out. Being able to define your own marriage? That's literally what the last century has been all about. All the social changes—the whole trajectory of the twentieth century, and the twenty-first century so far—when you boil it all down, what it's really about is you and me, every one of us, being able to decide for ourselves how we want to live our lives. It's no longer up to our parents, or decided by our religion, or dictated by our communities and our government. *We* get to decide how we want to live our lives, all of us, as individuals. *You* get to decide. Rich straight white men have always been able to do that— they had the privilege to be able to choose their own destiny, to change or rewrite the rules whenever they wanted, but now more and more people can. And that is literally what this upcoming election is all about. I don't understand how more people can't *see* that, how everything we've all worked so long and hard to achieve, all the progress we've made—"

"Min?"

She nodded. "Right, sorry, I went off, didn't I? The point is, those aren't meaningless words, what I said before."

"Okay," I said, "so Kevin and I get to decide what our marriage means."

She nodded emphatically.

"What if we disagree?" I said.

"Then you compromise. You work it out."

I didn't say anything. I almost kicked another stack of stones, but at the last second, I decided not to. Down on the water, the seagulls still cawed, but now I heard another sound too: voices. It was Ruby and Nate, probably on the beach over below the deck, laughing about something. So back at the house, everyone else was waking up too.

"Kevin wants to have kids," I said to Min.

"Really?" she said, surprised. She knew how I felt about the dream-destroying little monsters. "But I thought you talked that all out."

55

"Well, yeah, *now* he says he doesn't want them. But he used to want them. I think he only says that now because he knows it's what I want."

"Kevin is a big boy. If he says he's okay not having kids, you should believe him."

"But the point is," I said, "don't I need to be open to the possibility? Isn't that what being married is all about? And I don't want to be open to that possibility. There are *lots* of possibilities I don't want to be open to. And there are other possibilities that maybe I *do* want to be open to that Kevin might not."

"Are we talking about sex?"

I had to think about that. Kevin and I had a pretty great sex life, but we were definitely monogamous—that was important to us both. Still, I also knew that we were both reasonable guys, and if one of us was ever truly unhappy, we'd figure something out.

"We're two guys," I said. "Sex is actually one of the things I'm worried least about."

"That's totally sexist, what you said there, but I'm going to let it slide for the time being. So it's not sex. Then what are you worried about?"

"Other than the kid thing? That's it, I'm not quite sure." I thought for another second. "I want to make a difference in the world—help the homeless and cure AIDS, that kind of thing. And I have these vague dreams about traveling. Getting lost in South America, hitchhiking through Europe, living in a remote lighthouse for a year—although I know that last one would probably be a complete disaster, cold and impractical, and not nearly as romantic as it seems."

Min smiled.

"And obviously I want to make it as a screenwriter," I said. "I mean, that's why Kevin and I moved to Los

Angeles, and I still haven't had any success at all, and the city has turned out to be something of a dystopian hell-hole. But I sure as hell don't want to give up on that dream yet, and maybe not ever."

Min nodded.

"You only live once, you can't take it with you, and all that?" I said. "I don't want to be the guy who goes to work, and comes home and sits in my plush media room watching other people do cool things, like the couples on *House Hunters* who sell everything and move to some great new city. There's a line in *The Glass Menagerie* where the main character, Tom—"

"I know who the main character in *The Glass Menagerie* is."

"Tom says, 'People go to the movies rather than moving. Hollywood characters are supposed to have all the adventures for everybody in America.' Which I absolutely love. It's, like, my favorite line of all time. I want to move too, not just go to the movies." I thought about it. "Although I do love movies, so I also wouldn't mind a plush media room. I also like *House Hunters*. Or at least *House Hunters International*."

Min rolled her eyes. "Is it my turn now? Can I talk?"

"I already know what you're going to say. You're going to say that Kevin is a great guy, which he totally is. I mean, I literally just told you how he moved to Los Angeles with me so I could pursue my dream of screenwriting. And all the other things I talked about, I can do them *with* him. If we do disagree about something, we really will work it out."

"Wow, I'm absolutely brilliant. So? What's your rebuttal?"

"I dunno," I said. "It seems too optimistic. Aren't you the one who's always saying the whole world is going to hell?"

"Oh, sure, in the big picture, the corporations and religious fundamentalists are going to screw us all. But on a micro level, I still have faith."

I laughed out loud. At this point, I was back to liking how well Min knew me, that we really understood each other.

"I think I know what the problem is," Min said.

"You usually do."

Min ignored me. "You're afraid to grow up. You're afraid of being an adult." She sighed. "Such a Millennial."

"I am *not*. I mean, I'm a Millennial, but I'm not afraid of growing up. I'm *already* grown up. I'm twenty-five years old!" I thought about it for a second. "I'm also sick to death of the whole man-child thing. You know, that you see now in almost every TV show and every movie? Yes, yes, you can't stay home and drink beer and play video games all day, how incredibly tragic. They seriously *do* need to grow up. But that's not what this is."

Min kept ignoring me. "And that's what marriage symbolizes: being an adult. So it stands to reason it's giving you pause."

I'm afraid to grow up? I thought. That couldn't possibly be right. Could it?

It did have the ring of truth. Min was actually pretty good at this, calling me on my shit. But it usually all worked out in the end, because I'd been known to call her on her shit too.

"Just so we're clear," I said, "I'm really not having second thoughts about the wedding. I mean, like, at *all*."

"I know that."

"We're just talking."

"I know that too."

"All that said," I said, "well, who the hell wants to grow old? As far as I can tell, it's all about not getting enough fiber, and ear wax removal systems, and cracked crowns not being covered by insurance, and how you need some sort of tool to scrape your tongue or you'll get bad breath. Oh, and then you die."

"There's a slight possibility you're dwelling on the negative."

"Not to hear my parents tell it. But you want to know the worse part? They don't have friends, they have dinner party guests. I don't know if they ever did, but they don't now. It makes me so sad."

"So you've said. But that's one thing you're never going to have to worry about—not having friends. As for the bad breath, well, that's a separate issue."

"I want my life to be special," I said.

Now I really had gotten down to the nub of it. It wasn't so much that I was worried about growing older, or even that Kevin would one day announce that he desperately wanted kids, so we'd have to work out some kind of compromise and we'd end up getting a corgi.

It was that the whole marriage thing meant I was getting closer and closer to the point where I had to either put up or shut up about the kind of life I was going to live.

"I'm being neurotic again," I said glumly, "aren't I?"

Min beamed. "In all honesty, these might be the least neurotic feelings you've ever had."

"Really?"

"Really."

We both fell silent, looking around at the jagged foundations of the ruins around us. Now they reminded me of shark fins sticking up from a roiling ocean of sword ferns. The wind blew, and I smelled something stinky coming from the direction of the beach—more than just seaweed.

"So," she said, "what do you think happened to them? The people of Amazing."

"Really?" I said.

"Are you kidding? A mystery involving a deserted town? This is totally your kind of thing."

Now I *loved* how well Min knew me.

"You know," I said, "it might surprise you, but I'm back to seriously considering the possibility of alien abduction."

"I think I'm going with a time vortex, like in that old episode of *Star Trek*. Can you not see it? The vortex opens, and all the people come out to investigate, and then they all get sucked into another dimension?"

Right then, I got a text from Kevin:

Where are you? Come back to the house. There's something you need to see.

A beached whale. That's what Kevin thought I needed to see.

It was down on the beach below the Amazing Inn, not very far from where we'd had the campfire the night before. We would've seen it then, which meant it must have washed up during the night.

It wasn't a gigantic whale, like those pictures you see of sperm whales or humpbacks washed up on long sandy beaches. This was a killer whale on a small rocky beach. Killer whales are mostly black with white patches—I'm pretty sure they're not whales at all, but actually a kind of porpoise—and they only ever get about twenty feet long. This one was even smaller than that, maybe ten feet long, which meant it had to be young.

It was partly still in the water, with gentle waves washing around it. But it was definitely dead, a massive bulk with sagging fins and a gigantic pink tongue hanging halfway out of its mouth, like when Jabba the Hut dies in *Return of Jedi*.

"Well, that's a bummer," I said as we all stood around the carcass. I knew whales were really intelligent, so I felt like I should be more sad. Part of it was the bloated tongue, which was disgusting, and part of it was also the teeth, which weren't quite as sharp as a shark's, but gave me a little bit of the creeps anyway, knowing creatures big enough to chomp me down whole were swimming around out in Puget Sound.

"Killer whales aren't really killers," Min said, somehow reading the expression on my face. "Sometimes they kill other whales, but they mostly eat salmon and seals. They've literally never killed a human being. That's why 'orca' is a much better name for them."

"I wonder why it beached itself," Ruby said.

"Whales beach themselves for all kinds of reasons," Min said. "Parasites, genetic mutations, injuries from predators. But I don't think this orca did beach itself. I think it died at sea, probably several days ago, then the tide washed it up. Look at its eyes. Look at the skin."

Min had a point: its eyes were definitely clouded over, and its fins were drooping.

"Oh!" Ruby said. "You're *right*."

Meanwhile, Vernie looked at me and rolled her eyes. (For all her wonderful qualities, I concede that Min can sometimes be a know-it-all.)

"What about the smell?" Kevin said.

No one said anything for a second. The smell had been there all along, but it was only now registering.

Really registering.

It's not like it was the worst thing I'd ever smelled, a collapsed cesspool or something like that. But it wasn't roses either. Yes, I know a whale is a mammal not a fish, but it *smelled* like fish.

Dead fish.

A *lot* of dead fish. Or maybe just one really, really big dead fish.

Something occurred to me: this whale smelled pretty bad, and it had only been there for a few hours, maybe even less. I hadn't smelled it from the deck earlier that morning, and I had a feeling I would've noticed if it had been down here.

What's it going to be like in another twenty-four hours? I thought.

I felt guilty again, confronted by the death of this magnificent, probably-sentient creature, and here I was thinking mostly about the smell. But the fact is, this had the potential to ruin our wedding.

Sure enough, Kevin said, "We need to move it. Someone help me." He leaned over, and Nate and Gunnar immediately bent down to join him.

"You can't *move* it," Min said, horrified.

"Why not?" Nate said.

"Because it's illegal! This beached orca is an essential part of the marine ecosystem. As it decomposes, it will support of a whole array of life."

"It'll still be an essential part of the marine ecosystem supporting a whole array of life," Kevin said. "It'll just be doing it a little farther down the beach."

"No, it won't, mate," Nate said. "It's too damn heavy."

"How much do you think it weighs?" Kevin asked.

"Probably a thousand pounds," Gunnar said, somehow having already looked it up on his phone. "Huh. Infant mortality is extremely high. Up to fifty percent of all orcas die in the first seven months of life. Oh, and this is cool! Orcas can live to over a hundred years old! But they only live a quarter that long in captivity. Did you guys see that documentary, *Blackfish*?"

"Let's all try," Kevin said, ignoring Gunnar, still talking about moving the creature.

So we all tried (even Min, which I gave her credit for, considering we were probably committing a major crime). The black skin felt really cool to the touch and had this rubbery texture. As for the whale itself, it was almost surreally heavy. It was like trying to push several tons of wet towels all piled in a heap, somehow both loose and solid at the same time. Even all of us together couldn't budge it.

Finally, we gave up.

Not far away, seagulls stood on the rocky beach, eyeing the carcass.

"Maybe the tide'll take it away?" Kevin said hopefully.

"Maybe," Min said, but I could tell from the stark expression on both her and Gunnar's faces that there was virtually no chance of that.

"Well, maybe it's not so bad up on the porch," I said, trying to stay positive.

But if anything, the smell was even worse at the top of the stairs. It was like the breeze off the water lifted it right up to the deck.

I didn't know what to say to Kevin. I'd said the night before that nothing was going to go wrong with our wedding, but now something had. As long as that whale was down on the beach, there was no way we could get married at the Amazing Inn.

CHAPTER FIVE

"This is a *disaster*," Kevin said.

We were still on the deck, above the dead killer whale—er, orca—down on the beach.

"It's not a *disaster*," I said. "We could get, like, citronella candles."

"Absolutely," Min said, nodding.

"A perfect solution!" Vernie said.

But even as we stood there, the breeze blew, washing another cloud of dead whale stink up around us like an ocean wave. Vernie coughed, almost choking, even as she tried valiantly to suppress it. It didn't seem possible that the smell could have gotten so much worse in the last few minutes, but maybe it was more obvious now that we weren't focused on moving the whale.

"How is it not disaster?" Kevin said to me. "We can't possibly have the wedding here."

"So we'll just have everyone stay inside," I said, waltzing toward the house.

"Totally," Gunnar said.

"Hells to the yes!" Otto said.

Everyone followed me into the house.

You could even smell it inside the house with the doors closed. I also realized the dead whale must have been what I smelled all the way over in Amazing.

"It's not that bad, mate," Nate said to Kevin.

"No," Ruby said. "Really not bad at all."

Everyone was lying. I knew it and Kevin knew it. And the other thing that went unsaid was: This was how bad that dead orca smelled *now*. How much worse would it be twenty-four hours from now, after sitting in the sun all day?

I spotted Vernie and something occurred to me.

I stepped closer. "*This* is a movie moment," I said. "Isn't it?"

"What?" she said.

"The orca down on the beach. And the fact that the smell is so bad that we can't possibly hold the wedding here."

She thought about it. "I hate to admit it, but I think you're right."

If this had been a scene in a screenplay I was writing, I considered how I'd have my characters solve the problem.

"We need to find another wedding venue," I said to the group.

"Twenty-four hours before the ceremony?" Kevin said, agitated. "On an island? With a budget of zero?"

He was officially freaking out.

But that was okay. That was the great thing about being in a couple: if one person freaked out, there was still one person left to stay in control and try to make things right.

"It's a big island," I said. "There's got to be someplace we can have a wedding."

"Yes," Min said. "Let's see what we can find."

"Absolutely," Otto said again, nodding.

We all started moving for the door, but Vernie stayed where she was.

I looked back at her.

"You folks go," she said. "I think I'll stay here."

"Really?" I said, disappointed, but she nodded.

"I think I'll stay here too," Gunnar said matter-of-factly.

I looked at Min.

"I'd say he wants to take pictures of the orca," she muttered under her breath, "but knowing Gunnar, he's probably still more interested in the rain gutters."

Min, Otto, Kevin, Ruby, Nate, and I drove into town together, all jammed into Kevin's and my rental car. Kevin drove, and I called the local caterer we'd hired and explained the situation. I felt weird about mentioning the actual reason—a stinky beached orca—so I decided to leave that part out and say we had a plumbing problem.

"That's terrible!" she said. "Sure, I can think of a few places you might be able to call."

"Even with no money?" I said.

"Oh, don't worry about that," she said. "This is Vashon island! There's a little thing here we like to call the Vashon Groove—everything is always very laid-back. When you explain the situation, I'm sure someone will be happy to help you out."

I jotted down the numbers she gave me, already feeling better. It *was* the island, after all. Like I said before, Vashon Island had a reputation for being artsy and eccentric. If you were a by-the-numbers, type-A personality, you weren't going to be very happy on an island where the roads often weren't marked and you were totally dependent on the coming and going of the ferry.

When I disconnected, I said to Kevin, "We're going to be fine."

Behind the wheel, he nodded stiffly.

I called the places she'd given me—the grange, the art museum, and something called The Old Fruit Barreling Plant—but it turned out that both the grange and art museum were already booked, and no one ever picked up at the fruit barreling plant (and there was no voicemail).

"Well?" Kevin said when I hung up the phone the third time. This might have been a little bitchy on his part, because he had to know from listening that I hadn't had any luck.

"It's okay," I said, still determined not to add fuel to his freak-out fire. "We'll find a place, don't worry."

The town of Vashon was located at a crossroads right in the middle of the island. The town itself was sort of a crossroads too, split almost fifty-fifty between practical businesses for the islanders, like the hardware store, the grocery store, and the post office, and funkier places for the tourists and the artsy crowd, like the store with an olive oil tasting bar, and a gallery where the art was made from nothing but stuff that washed up on the beach (I suspect they cheated). I also spotted not one but *two* marijuana stores.

Basically, Vashon was an overalls-and-dreadlocks kind of town.

Kevin parked the car and we all climbed out to look around. It was late in the year, well past the tourist season, but the streets were pretty crowded.

"Now what?" Kevin said.

It was actually a good question. I'd been acting as if by driving into town the answer would become obvious, like a bush would start burning and announce the perfect alternative wedding venue. But even if the Vashon Groove was a real thing, I couldn't imagine any of the restaurants in town letting us use their backrooms for a wedding, not without paying them (a lot) for the privilege. So what to do?

Saturday happened to be the day of the island farmers' market, which was taking place in a vacant lot along the main street.

"Let's check that out," I said, pointing.

We reached the market, which was mobbed, and started walking the aisles, past booths and tables with homemade cheeses and artisan breads, and assortments of local vegetables—mostly leafy green stuff like kale and spinach, and lots of pumpkins and squashes. The booth selling free-range eggs didn't just have chicken eggs, they also had duck, goose, quail, ostrich, emu, and "heirloom," which I was pretty sure was another kind of chicken.

I passed a table selling marijuana in all its glorious forms—buds, joints, pills, brownies, chocolate, topical oils, and, of course, gummy bears. (I wanted to say, "What, no marijuana Swedish fish?" but I didn't have the nerve.)

"Island grown!" called the man behind the booth—plump and ruddy-faced.

"I've read about this," Min said to me. "Since marijuana was legalized here in Washington, Vashon Island farmers are trying to become sort of the Napa Valley of pot."

"There's just one problem," said the man behind the table. "The only way off the island is by air or by sea—both of which are regulated by the federal government, which still considers marijuana illegal."

"Oh, that's interesting!" I said. "So what do you do?"

"Make damn sure we don't get a Republican president!"

Min immediately perked up. "Exactly! I don't know why more people can't see how it's all connected—how the issues *matter*. But no, we have to make *our* elections all about personality."

"Russel?" Kevin said, growing impatient.

"Right!" I said. We really did have a tight time-limit.

I forged onward, but now I noticed that people were glancing our way.

People are staring at Otto, I thought. It happened every time I was out in public with him, and it pissed me off how obvious people could be, how oppressive it felt. At least it wasn't very often that people actually said insulting things—called him a freak or anything like that.

Someone stepped right in front of him.

"You're Otto Digmore," the woman said.

"Yeah," Otto said.

"I love you on *Hammered.*"

All around us, eyes brightened and smiles blossomed. People were staring at Otto, but not for the reason I'd thought. They recognized him from his television show.

"Can I get your autograph?" someone else said.

"Sure," Otto said, as smooth and graceful as all the celebrities I'd seen living in Los Angeles. He even carried his own pen.

He started signing things—papers and pamphlets, a rolling paper someone had just bought at the marijuana booth. And of course everyone wanted a selfie with him. Best of all, no one said anything stupid or patronizing like, "I can't believe how *brave* you are!"

I was sort of in awe of how Otto managed all this, how non-flustered he was. Before I knew it, his crowd was even bigger than the one around the old-fashioned cider press up ahead, where people were juicing their own apples. In spite of my stress about the wedding, I couldn't help but take a moment and appreciate how incredibly cool it was that my friend was an actual celebrity, especially since he was a person who had spent almost all of his life drawing stares for exactly the opposite reason.

As quickly as it started, Otto tried to wrap things up.

"Okay, thanks a lot," he said, quietly, but firmly. "I've got to go now."

As most of the people drifted away, I leaned in close to him. "I'm so impressed!" I said. "Look, that guy is filming us with his phone. Wave! One trip to the farmers' market and you're going to be all over social media."

He groaned.

I looked at him. "What's wrong with that?"

"Nothing, it doesn't matter."

"No, seriously."

"Russel, it's nothing. Let's just find you a place for your wedding."

"Wedding?" someone said. It wasn't the guy who was filming us, or anyone Otto had signed an autograph for, but someone who'd been passing by. He was loaded down with cloth sacks full of stuff from the market.

I stared, trying to decide if I wanted to tell him what we were talking about. I was pretty sure he wasn't one of Otto's stalkers.

And, well, he wasn't unattractive either. He was older, in his thirties, tall and reasonably brawny. His face was unshaven, and his hair grew long, but not unkempt. His shirt and jeans were old and faded, only a cut or two above "homeless," but that wasn't that unusual here on the island.

"My boyfriend and I are getting married tomorrow," I said, nodding toward Kevin. "But we can't do it where we thought, so now we have to find somewhere else on the island to hold a wedding for sixty-seven guests."

"I have a place," he said.

I sensed my friends all looking at each other, curious. Meanwhile, I glanced at Kevin. He seemed as intrigued-but-skeptical as I felt.

"And we don't have any money," I said to the man.

He laughed. "That doesn't matter. We'd be glad to have you. It's our barn. We're an intentional community."

Most people might have been taken aback by the words "intentional community," like he was talking about a commune or something. But even if he was, I didn't care. Two years earlier, Min had briefly considered herself polyamorous. And back in high school, I'd sort of dated a guy in a commune. True, some of his friends turned out to be eco-terrorists, and people had almost died because of them, but that's a whole other story.

The point is, it took a lot to shock me.

"A barn, huh?" I said. That was the real sticking point here, not the commune. Who wanted to hold their wedding in a barn?

"It's not like it sounds," he said. "We have a couple of animals, but we can move them out for the wedding. And it's clean. It doesn't smell. We've held weddings there before."

Given that the only alternative venue right now included six tons of rotten sushi, I liked the sound of that a lot.

"You're really serious about this?" Kevin asked him.

"Sure, why not?" the man said. "Hey, it's the Vashon Groove."

So this *was* a real thing.

I exchanged another look with Kevin. The skepticism in his eyes was mostly gone now, swept away like cobwebs in an attic.

I looked from Min to Otto to Ruby, all questioning them with my eyes to see if they agreed this was a good idea. (I didn't look at Nate, because I didn't care what he thought.)

Everyone seemed to agree that we should at least check it out.

"I'm Russel," I said to the man. "And this is Kevin." I introduced the rest of our little group too. Everyone grinned stupidly, even Min.

"I'm Duane," the man said, and somehow he even made *that* name sound sexy. "Do you guys wanna come out and take a look right now?"

"Sure," I said. "Where are you parked?"

In our car, Kevin followed Duane across some back roads, then down a twisty gravel road through some woods. It was a little like the road to the Amazing Inn, except we were in the interior of the island, not anywhere near the beach.

The trees fell away, and we found ourselves in the middle of a couple of acres of grassy hills. Ducks and geese floated lazily on a little pond, and I spotted a pretty impressive vegetable garden, though it looked pretty picked over. At the end of the road, a large green farmhouse loomed, alongside, yes, a big barn that had clearly been restored.

I don't want to overstate things: the house was a little dumpy, and I saw rusted cars here and there. But all in all, it was pretty seriously charming.

"What *is* this place?" Min said.

"It's perfect," Kevin said. "That's what it is!"

I was agreeing with him, even as I was also thinking: *This seems* too *perfect. What's the catch?* Angry ghosts like that farmhouse in *The Conjuring*? A band of violent local rapists like in *Straw Dogs*? It really did seem too good to be true.

We parked the car and all climbed out. The air smelled like cut grass and drying leaves, and over on the pond, a goose honked.

The barn greeted us like a giant Buddha: big, fat, and welcoming. The outside was done in cedar, still so new that it had barely begun to fade. The big doors were open, and the inside beckoned, bright and clean. It was easily big enough for sixty-seven people!

In the barn, a goat bleated, but it sounded rustic and adorable, not annoying.

Duane walked back toward us from his car, a grin etched onto his bristly face. "Whadaya think?"

I looked at Kevin, who was beaming like I needed to wear sunglasses.

"I don't know what to say," I said. "It looks perfect."

"Fantastic," Duane said.

Two people stepped out onto the wrap-around front porch of the farm house, a man and a woman—older than Duane, probably in their forties or fifties, both a bit chubby.

The man was wearing tighty-whities and the woman was completely naked.

They waved—very friendly, even if it made the woman's breasts and the man's fat wiggle.

Tentatively, we all waved back.

Then we looked at Duane.

"Oh, right," he said. "We're a clothing-optional community." He didn't say this like he'd been hiding it from us and now wanted to get some kind of prurient thrill by shocking us. It was more like he'd forgotten. "I hope that's okay."

As we were driving away from the farm, it was impossible not to laugh.

"I would've loved to see your mom there!" Min said to me. "Can you imagine?"

"I know!" I said, even as I also thought, *It meant I would've gotten to see Duane naked.*

But alas, having our wedding in Duane's barn really was out of the question. If it had only been Kevin's and my close friends, that would have been one thing, but we had a lot of our relatives coming. We knew most of them had never been to a same-sex wedding before, and the last thing we wanted was to make people feel even more uncomfortable. Yes, yes, our wedding was all about us, it was *our* day, about whatever *we* wanted. But come on.

I noticed that Kevin wasn't laughing with the rest of us.

"You okay?" I asked him, looking across the car with Min between us.

He clenched the steering wheel.

Finally he turned to me. "What about a church?"

"What about it?" I said.

"For the wedding. Maybe we could find an actual church."

No one said anything for a second, and I thought it was funny that it wasn't until now that anyone had even *considered* holding our wedding in an actual church, despite the fact that this was where weddings were usually held.

On the other hand, it's not like we were crazy. Given what complete babies most churches had been on the subject of same-sex marriage over the last few years, who could blame us? Why in the world would we want to go somewhere we weren't welcome—or, in some churches, where we're now maybe sometimes grudgingly tolerated.

Thanks, but no thanks.

(Plus, there was the fact that neither Kevin nor I was religious. I was raised Catholic, but it never really took. It was partly the anti-gay thing, but that was only part of it. By the time I was fourteen, religion mostly seemed silly, like believing that the characters in *The Lord of the Rings* are real. But I tried hard not to stereotype, because I knew reasonable people who thought otherwise.)

Min looked up all the Vashon Island churches on her phone. "Well, the Catholics are out, obviously. And the evangelicals, and anything with the word 'gospel' or 'bible' in it. Forget the Methodists and the Mormons.

"The wedding is tomorrow at three," I said. "We don't have that many guests, only sixty..."

I stopped in mid-word. Something flickered on the woman's face. Had I said something wrong? Had Nate and Ruby moved on from the labyrinth to somehow destroying the church itself? I glanced behind me, but they didn't seem to be doing any more damage than before.

I turned back to her. "What's wrong?" I said. I didn't dare look at Kevin.

"*This* weekend?" she said. "I'm so sorry, I didn't know it was this weekend."

"What's wrong with this weekend?" I said.

She hemmed and hawed. "It's nothing, really. I mean, so what if there are bats in the bell tower? They've been there for months. They're an important part of the island ecosystem! I don't understand what the big deal is—it's not like they can get inside the church."

"You *literally* have bats in your belfry?" Min said.

"Technically, rabid bats. Or rabid *bat*. There's only been one so far, at least that we know of."

We all instinctively glanced up at the tower to the church—and sort of recoiled. Rabid bats were a *huge* deal. Did this woman really not know that?

"What are they going to do, kill all the bats on the whole island?" the woman was saying. "Anyway, the bat removal guys won't be out on the island again until Monday."

"Is there another church on the island that you think would help us?" Kevin asked.

"Of course! The Unitarians for sure. They use the community church."

The Presbyterians could go either way, and so could the Lutherans, and I'm not sure we want to deal with that." She looked up. "Can I just say how incredibly depressing this is?" She looked back at her phone. "Wait! The Episcopalians! They're a bunch of raging liberals, right?"

"I think so," Otto said.

Min did some research on her phone. "Individual pastors have discretion," she said. "They can refuse to marry gay couples if they want. Which is, of course, such a principled position for the church to take, like how when society decided it was wrong that restaurants were allowed to refuse service to black people, we all then agreed to let individual restaurants continue to discriminate. Or, wait, *no, we didn't!* Because everyone realized *that would be incredibly bigoted*."

I laughed and realized that even though Min could be a little sanctimonious, I almost always agreed with her politics.

"They won't refuse us," I said. "Come on, it's Vashon Island! The way this island seems so far, they probably all take a toke on sacramental bong."

We found the Episcopal church in a wooded area right along one of the main roads.

"Oh, cool," Otto said, pointing to a sign. "They have a labyrinth."

"A what?" Nate said.

"It's a kind of circular maze," Min explained.

We parked in the church lot (empty except for two other cars). The church itself was modern-ish, made of dark wood—a big rectangle of a building with a front grill-like covering over stained-glass windows. A narrow steeple, another rectangle, rose up on one side.

Nate and Ruby immediately made a beeline for the labyrinth, which was located in the grass in front of the building. Naturally, I'd been expecting some sort of massive hedge maze, like in *Harry Potter and the Goblet of Fire*. Instead, it was just a circular pathway made of gravel cut into the patchy lawn. It started at the edge of the circle, and you could follow the pathway around and around until you reached a flower-like thingy in the very middle. The whole labyrinth wasn't more than twenty-five feet across.

"I confess to feeling more than a little disappointed," I said.

"It's supposed to be contemplative," Min said. "You walk the labyrinth and ponder the nature of existence."

"And, see, I was expecting more in the way of minotaurs and burning goblets."

"Race you?" Nate said to Ruby.

"Oh, you're *on*, Kangaroo Jack," Ruby said, and they both sprinted for the start of this little gravel pathway that was only about eight inches wide. Which meant, of course, that they immediately ran into each other, and the whole "race" was the two of them trying to drag each other off the path.

"What the hell?" Nate said, laughing. "Have you gone troppo?"

I knew he and Ruby were completely missing the point of the labyrinth, and Min and I even sort of shook our heads at each other, but the truth is, I was jealous that the two of them were so easily able to cut loose and have fun.

"Help you folks?" came a voice behind us.

Kevin, Min, Otto, and I all turned.

It was a middle-aged woman with a weathered b friendly face. Everything about her was sensible—h short hair, the shoes, the no-nonsense jersey.

"Oh!" I said. "You're with the church? You're ju who we wanted to see."

"You *dog*!" shrieked Ruby, mid-labyrinth. "Y cheating dog!"

"Bloody hell!" Nate said.

The woman eyed Nate and Ruby, who were basic destroying the church's contemplative labyrinth their frenzied battle royale to the end. I could only h the woman wouldn't hold it against us.

She looked at us very drolly.

Come on! I wanted to say. *It's a dumb gravel pathw some dead grass.*

"We're getting married," I said, "but there was a blem with the location. We need a new venue, bu don't have much money." I stepped closer to Kevir took his hand, to make sure there wasn't any confu about the fact that we were a gay couple. I didn't her to be shocked and appalled—at her own discr of course!—when she realized I wasn't actually m ing Min.

Seeing us together, her face brightened like a C mas tree. She'd completely forgotten about Nat Ruby.

"Oh, that's *terrible*!" she said. "Of course! We'c to help you. Anything at all, we'll make it work."

I looked at Min and grinned. I'd been right abc Vashon Episcopalians being crazy-eyed liberals. could actually *see* Kevin relaxing, the tension leavi body like he was unwinding a scarf. I kind of war kiss him right there, but I didn't want to pu woman past her point of tolerance.

Kevin and I both froze, unsure how to react or exactly what to feel.

"There's just one problem," the woman said. "Since our church is closed, the Community Church is where we've moved all *our* activities tomorrow afternoon."

Kevin was back to looking pretty gloomy, and I didn't want him taking us all down in his own car-crash suicide, so I decided to handle the driving from that point on.

"It's going to be okay," I said. "We'll find a place. We've got plenty of time."

"Why couldn't we have the wedding on a beach somewhere?" Nate asked.

"Old people," I said. "We need bathrooms." Both Kevin and I had elderly relatives coming to the wedding. "Plus, what if it rains?"

At that, I glanced out the window to one side. Unfortunately, it did look like it was starting to cloud up.

But that's when my eyes fell upon a public park.

"Stop the car!" I said, even though I was the one driving.

"A park?" Kevin said. "You want to have our wedding in a park?"

"Well, it's not my first choice," I said, "but there *are* bathrooms. And there's a covered area if it rains." I looked at Kevin and smiled. "Hey, our relationship began in a picnic shelter, right? The stinky picnic gazebo?"

He sort of nodded while all six of us took it all in. The picnic shelter was surprisingly large—so big it might even fit sixty-seven guests. As for the location, it was right on the water, with a view looking down into a quiet little bay. It was actually kinda sorta spectacular.

But I didn't want to get my hopes up again just yet.

We walked deeper into the park, examining it like furniture in a showroom.

We entered the picnic shelter.

"Electrical outlets," Ruby said, pointing. "For, like, the caterer? And I bet we could buy some simple space heaters at the hardware store."

"We could get some nice decorations too," Min said.

"What if someone's already using it?" Kevin said.

"In September?" Nate said.

"Min and I can come here early and stake it out," Ruby said.

Then Min said, "There's a problem."

I stepped closer. She was pointing to a sign that said, *This area is available for reservation. Parties of fifteen or more must register with the Vashon Parks Department.* And it gave a phone number and an address.

I tried the phone number, but nobody was answering.

"It's a Saturday," Kevin said. "They're probably closed."

"Maybe so," I said, "but let's go stop by the office just in case."

The office of the Vashon Parks Department was in this little office park on the outskirts of town. It was two stories, only five businesses total—lawyers and accountants, that type of thing. There were cars in the parking lot, which I took to be a good sign, but all the blinds were down, so it didn't look like anything was open.

A woman stepped out of one of the offices on the second floor, onto a wooden deck. She was locking up.

"There!" Kevin said. "I bet that's it!" Sure enough, by this point, I could see the words painted on the window: Vashon Parks Department.

I slammed on the brakes, parking the car haphazardly in a stall, and Kevin, Min, Otto, and I ran for the stairs, meeting the woman halfway down.

"Thank God we caught you!" I said. Somehow I was out of breath, even though I'd only run about twenty feet from the car. I guess it was all the excitement of getting there in time.

She stopped on the stairs, peering down at us like a cat we'd just woken from its nap.

"We're getting married tomorrow," I said quickly, "but there's a problem with the place we rented. We desperately need a new location, so we wanted to reserve the picnic shelter at Jensen Point."

She kept staring at us. If she was still a cat, she might have started licking herself—completely indifferent. Up close, I got a better look at her now. She was younger than most of the other people we'd met on the island, in her twenties, and blond and wearing make-up, but somehow drabber than everyone else. Or maybe it was only the fact that the sun had clouded over by now.

"Or any park," Kevin said. "Anywhere at all, really."

She stared at us a second longer, licking her imaginary paws.

Then she said, "The office is closed. I just locked up."

We looked at her, then up at the office again. There couldn't have been more than ten feet between them. The set of keys that she'd used to lock the door was still dangling in her hand.

On the other hand, her knuckles were white, like she was squeezing those keys tightly.

"Well," Min said, "do you think you could maybe unlock it again for us?"

All four of us smiled oh-so-sweetly.

"Unfortunately, the office closes at noon on Saturdays," the woman said.

I couldn't help glancing down at my phone. It read 12:02 p.m.

She started down the stairs again. We had no choice but to step to one side to let her pass, not without being, like, abusive jerks.

"But..." I started to say. *What about the Vashon Groove?* That's what I almost said, but I couldn't figure out if it would help or hurt our cause.

She didn't stop, just sauntered for her car.

"Please!" I said. "We're desperate!"

She didn't even hesitate. She opened the door to her car and slid inside. She hadn't unlocked it with a key or a beeper or anything. I guess that was another part of living on an island: no one bothered with locks. But at least she hadn't closed the door yet.

"Well, is it okay if we use the park without a permit?" I asked. "We only have thirty guests." Yes, I was lying a bit.

If she was a cat, now I was the mouse. "Do it and you're looking at a thousand-dollar fine," she said. "And don't think they don't patrol the parks on Sundays, because they do!"

"But what about the Vashon Groove?" I blurted. At this point, what did I have to lose?

Naturally, she slammed her car door in my face.

CHAPTER SIX

Back in the car, Kevin did a pretty good imitation of the dead orca: he was saggy and lifeless, like another mound of wet towels sitting in the seat next to me.

I felt bad too, but with Kevin so down, I wanted to go on being the non-freaked-out one—the supportive boyfriend who keeps saying that everything will work out in the end.

"Maybe we could do it at my parents' house," I said. "The wedding, I mean."

"Back on the mainland?" Kevin said.

"Well, yeah," I said, even as I was thinking: *What would my mom think of that?* She'd never been supportive of my being gay, and like I said about churches, who wants to hold a wedding in a place where you're sort of grudgingly tolerated? It also wasn't a very big house. Would it even *fit* that many people? Kevin's parents' house was even smaller.

Still, what was the alternative? Cancel the wedding? I already mentioned how the ceremony itself was kind of a formality. All we really needed was for Min to sign a piece of paper, and then we'd be married. But what about what Kevin had said the night before about how a wedding was a chance for a couple to tell their friends how much they loved each other? If we didn't have an actual ceremony, would anyone take *us* seriously?

Kevin didn't answer, just turned and stared out the window again.

When we got home, we all climbed out of the car and headed for the house. But while the others disappeared inside, I lingered outside with Kevin.

"What do you want to do?" I asked him.

"You mean should we cancel?" he said.

I nodded. "It's early enough that we could send out an email."

Kevin sniffed the air. "Do you smell that?"

"I know, I know. Look, I really think we should make a decision."

"No, seriously." Kevin looked at me. "Smell the air."

I took a whiff, but I didn't smell anything.

I looked at Kevin quizzically. Then I let myself feel the tiniest smidgen of hope.

We entered the house. Everyone was out on the deck, clustered at the edge of it, looking down on the beach. The door to the outside was open, but I still couldn't smell any dead whale.

We joined our friends on the deck.

Yup, still no dead whale smell.

I looked back at Kevin, who looked confused, but more hopeful than ever.

Our friends were turning to us—Min, Otto, Nate, and Ruby—smiles plastered on their faces.

"What's going on?" I asked.

"It's gone," said Min.

87

"The whale?"

Everyone nodded, even as they smirked.

Kevin and I hurried to the edge of the deck, scanning the beach below us. There was an indention in the rocks and sand, a big one, but no orca.

"Was it the tide?" Kevin asked. It had definitely come in a bit.

But no one seemed to know.

Behind us, Vernie stepped out onto the porch. "You're back," she said. "How did it go?"

"Vernie!" I said. "What happened to the whale?"

"Whale?"

"It's gone!"

"It *is*? That's wonderful! I didn't see, I was in taking a nap."

Gunnar appeared next to Vernie on the deck. He was carrying a shoebox full of shelf fungus that he'd apparently collected in the woods outside the house.

"Did you know that before 1969, fungi were considered part of the plant kingdom?" he said. "Now, of course, they're considered their own kingdom, because they're completely different from plants. In a lot of ways, they're actually more like animals, absorbing their food using digestive enzymes."

I was immediately suspicious.

"Gunnar," I said, "what happened to the whale on the beach?"

He looked confused, but only for a second. "Oh, I got rid of it." He glanced at Min. "And don't worry, I did move it farther down the beach, to a place where there aren't any houses, so it wouldn't bother anyone."

"But...*how*?" she said.

It wasn't often that I saw Min speechless, but I couldn't really appreciate it, because I was speechless too. We all were. We'd seen the orca—we'd *touched* it. We'd all been convinced it was impossible to move.

Gunnar offered us an indifferent shrug. "Don't worry about it. It's all taken care of, and everything is okay. Think of it as my wedding gift to you guys. I wanted to make sure the ceremony went off okay."

With that, he turned and went inside to categorize his fungi.

I knew it was pointless to try and get Gunnar to tell us how he'd moved the whale. He acted like he was indifferent about the whole thing, but I think some part of him was enjoying our confusion. Back in school, he'd been teased and bullied a lot for being different. Since then, he'd decided to own his weirdness, and I think he'd also come to enjoy confounding people. He'd sort of made it his personal brand.

A few minutes later, I found Kevin in our bedroom sitting on the bed.

I closed the door behind me. "You okay?" I said.

"I'm sorry I freaked out back there," he said. "I actually thought we might have to cancel the wedding."

I sat down next to him. "Can I just say how glad I am that for the first time in our relationship, you're being the neurotic one? Is this like with Gunnar—your wedding gift to me?"

Kevin didn't smile. He was seriously upset about this.

I scooted closer so our hips were purposely touching. We'd turned the heat off in the bedroom when we left that morning, and now I could feel the warmth of his body.

"You didn't freak out," I said. "Or if you did, it was a good thing. It makes me happy that you're taking our wedding so seriously. But here's why I didn't freak out. The wedding itself doesn't matter. I love you, and I'm going to spend the rest of my life with you. And I don't need a piece of paper, or a ceremony, or anything at all to know that."

"I know. I feel the same way. But..."

"What?" He didn't answer, so I said, "Come on, tell me."

"I don't know why I want us to have an actual wedding, or why I want it to be perfect, but I do." He thought for a second. "Do you remember that story Gunnar told about my introducing myself to the class back in the seventh grade?"

I nodded.

"I was telling the truth when I said it was all an act," he said. "I was terrified."

"I bet. Joining a new school in the middle of the year? I wouldn't wish that on my enemy." I'd always hated it when adults mocked kids' problems. Years later, I still remembered exactly how difficult the seventh grade was, and whenever adults made fun of that, it always seemed to me to be yet another kind of cruelty.

"But it all worked out," I said. "No one knew you were nervous, and you went on to be the most popular kid in class."

"It didn't work out. It was a disaster."

I looked at him.

"Sure, I was popular," he said, "but only because I lied about who I was. I played sports and told jokes and flirted with all the girls, including the teachers. But I was a gay kid with a crush on Mr. Johnson, and an eye on the cute redheaded boy over by the window." This made me smile, because I *had* sat by the window in the seventh grade. Kevin hadn't been lying the night before when he said he noticed me. "I was terrified that someone would figure it out. I don't think I ever relaxed the whole time I was in school, not until I finally talked to you in the park that night all those years later."

I nodded again. Kevin made a good point: just because something looks perfect, that doesn't mean it is.

"Our wedding isn't the same thing," I said.

"I know. But these last few years have been so crazy. First, I break up with Colin. Then my career goes completely to shit."

I couldn't help feeling guilty about this. Kevin had broken up with Colin because of me (long story). His career had gone to shit because of me too—because I'd wanted to move to Los Angeles to pursue my dream of screenwriting.

Kevin saw on my face what I was thinking.

"None of it is your fault," he said. "I don't regret any of it, not at all. If I had to do it over again, I wouldn't change a thing."

Except for the way it ended with Colin, I thought. I knew Kevin was thinking this too. Neither of us had acted very nobly there.

"But sometimes it sort of feels like my life has spun out of my control," Kevin said, "like the things that happen aren't ever what I expect them to be. So then came this wedding, and I thought, 'Finally! Something I *can* control.'"

"You know they literally say that's not true about weddings, right? That you can plan them, but you can't *control* them. That to enjoy them, you have to sort of let them go."

"I know! All this is stupid, I know that."

"It's not stupid. It makes sense. In fact, I know exactly what you're talking about. I had an image of this weekend too."

Kevin looked at me.

"You know how I wanted our good friends here all weekend?" I said. "I guess I thought they'd come, and they'd all be these adoring little puppies, perfectly arranged for us to pet and coo over. It didn't occur to me that they all have their own lives, their own things going on, their own concerns."

And Kevin too, I thought. I hadn't expected him to be so distracted this weekend.

"But maybe it's better this way," I went on. "We're spending the weekend with real people, not fantasies. The truth is, we *don't* know what's going to happen. But I stand by what I said before: in the end, I think it'll all work out."

Kevin kept looking at me, but now his eyes were like windows with no curtains or blinds. I could see far enough inside to tell that he was impressed.

"Have I mentioned how much I like you?" he said.

"You have. But not lately."

"I like you."

"How much on a scale of one to ten?"

"Fifty zillion."

I considered this for a second. "I guess that'll do."

Later, Ruby found some kayaks and wetsuits—Puget Sound was too cold to swim in without a wetsuit even in summer, much less autumn. I wasn't sure where Ruby had found the equipment. Out in the garage? I didn't remember Christie saying anything about any kayaks, but if they hadn't been locked up, I had to assume they were okay to use. Ruby invited everyone back down to the beach to give them a go, which did sound fun. Plus, I wanted to check and make sure the whale hadn't somehow floated back.

I looked at Vernie, seated in the living room. "Whaddaya say?" I asked her.

"Oh, you go," she said. She nodded to her Kindle. "I'm right in the middle of a good book."

I felt guilty that it seemed like Vernie wasn't really fitting in with everyone else. Had I made a mistake by inviting her for the whole weekend?

"Nah," I said, "I think I'll hang out up here too."

By now, everyone else had mostly left for the beach, and Vernie said, "Oh, please! You are *not* staying behind to babysit me."

"I'm *not*," I said. "I thought of another idea for a single-location script, and I wanted your opinion."

Vernie glared at me. "I don't believe you."

"Well, it's true. Let me get a cup of tea, and I'll tell you all about it."

I went into the kitchen, but mostly I was stalling for time. I *had* stayed behind to keep Vernie company, and I *didn't* have another single-location screenplay idea.

I returned to the front room with two cups of steeping tea—and absolutely no idea what I was going to say.

"Well?" Vernie said.

I smiled stupidly, wishing she'd have forgotten about the dumb screenplay idea and I could deftly try to change the subject.

But now I was stuck. I had to say *something*. Still, sometimes the most interesting ideas are the ones that come to you when you're under pressure.

"It's called *The Compound*, and it's a comedy," I said. "An old man dies, and his two sons inherit his farm— no, wait, it's a daughter and a son. It's big, but really isolated, way out in the middle of nowhere. The father spells out in his will that they can't sell the farm until they both live there together for a year."

I said that *sometimes* the most interesting ideas come to you when you're under pressure. This wasn't one of those times.

"Go on," Vernie said.

"Well," I said, stalling again, "the man wants to turn the farm into a commune and he invites all his dippy, free-love friends, but the woman wants to turn it into a right-wing militia, and she invites all her paranoid, gun-crazy friends. And somehow they all have to live together."

I thought about the words that had come out of my mouth. Obviously, it had been inspired by my experience with Duane and his clothing-optional commune, but I liked the addition of the right-wing militia sister. It wasn't a completely terrible idea.

Vernie thought about it too. "*The Compound*, huh? I like what you did with the genders, making the woman the conservative and the man liberal—switching up the stereotypes. It has potential, especially as a comedy. But is that really a single-location script? It seems like it's a single-setting, but there are a lot of different locations. How would that save the producers' any money?"

She was right, of course: it wasn't really a single-location script. Still, the point had been to distract Vernie, and it did seem to have been successful at that.

Vernie looked down at her mug of tea, blowing into it, cooling it, dissolving the rising steam. But the second she stopped blowing, the steam reformed.

"How are you doing?" I said. "Honestly."

She looked up at me. "What? I'm fine. What do you mean? I'm *great*."

Vernie wasn't fine. Something was bugging her, but this was my wedding weekend, and she didn't want to spoil it by bringing up anything heavy.

"How are *you*?" she said. "How are you doing with the whole wedding business?" Now she was the one deftly trying to change the subject.

But I thought about this. What if I told her the truth—that I did have some (very slight!) mixed emotions about the wedding? Maybe that would give her permission to be honest with me.

"It was strange earlier," I said, "when that whale washed up on the beach, and we thought the wedding might be canceled. I was sad, but mostly because I felt bad for Kevin."

"Oh?" she said.

I went on to tell her what I'd told Min: that I wasn't worried about getting married to *Kevin*, but that I was a little concerned about marriage in general. About how it often seemed to signal the start of when a person's life got boring.

"That won't happen," Vernie said.

"But I've heard you yourself say stuff like that," I said. "You told me once that when you lived in Los Angeles, you were always having to choose between going to your kids' soccer games and spending the weekend with Warren Beatty and Goldie Hawn."

This was true. Vernie had told me lots of stories about her life in Hollywood, and how her kids resented her to this day, because she had sometimes chosen her career over them.

"My marriage was different," she said.

"Different how?"

She sipped her tea, and now I wondered if *she* was stalling for time. "Just different."

It seemed like Vernie didn't want to talk about it, so I decided to change the subject a bit. "Min says I'm afraid of growing up," I said.

"Are you?"

"Probably."

"Good! You should be. Too many people *do* grow up and turn boring. There's absolutely no excuse for that at all. But part of me thinks those people couldn't have been all that interesting to begin with. So they got drunk and had a lot of sex on the weekend. Maybe they even got a tattoo! How does *that* make a person interesting?"

"What makes a person interesting?" I asked.

"When they're passionate about the things they love," she said without any hesitation at all. "The more passionate they are, the more interesting they are."

This answer was so typically Vernie. But the more I thought about it, the more obvious it seemed. It was definitely true for Gunnar, Min, Otto, and also Vernie herself.

"It's a choice, you know," she said. "Whether or not you become boring? It's not like they appear one day and put you in handcuffs. They don't *make* you be boring."

"Really?" I said. "I thought you turned thirty, and they forced you to stay home watching *House Hunters*."

"I love *House Hunters*," Vernie said. "Or at least *House Hunters International*."

"I know, me too!" I watched her a second longer. "Come on, tell me what's really going on."

She sipped her tea again. "Why do you keep thinking there's something going on?"

"Because I know you. And I have a feeling you don't want to tell me the truth because you think it'll put a damper on my wedding weekend. But the whole point of inviting my friends this weekend was to spend time with them. With you. The *real* you."

She stared at me, looking both amused and annoyed.

"So is that why you told me how you're having misgivings about the wedding?" she said. "To get me to lower my guard?"

Not misgivings exactly, I thought.

"And don't think I don't know you were stalling for time earlier," she went on, "and that you came up with that screenplay idea on the fly."

Vernie was smart, I had to give her that.

"You got me," I said. "But it's not like you're doing such a bang-up job of hiding your feelings either. Either you have to tell me what's really going on in your life, or you need to start doing a much better job of lying."

Vernie laughed, long and hearty, and I knew I'd finally broken through the wall.

"Oh, I wish it was something interesting," she said. "I wish I could say I had cancer or something. Would that make a great plot-reveal? I spend the whole weekend acting like everything's great, how happy I am for you, and then after I leave, you find out I only have six weeks left to live. Or is that a terrible cliché?"

"A terrible cliché," I said. "And also a terrible *joke*. I don't want you to have cancer!"

"Well, I don't. I'm healthy as a horse. No, it's far less interesting. I just feel old and irrelevant. I always feel this way in the fall, but for some reason, it's worse this year than usual."

"You're not *old*," I said, really trying to sell it.

"Are you kidding? I'm ancient. Plus, my kids hate me, I'm sleeping like shit, the studio is still screwing me on royalties, and the latest update on my operating system screwed up all the programs on my computer, including the drivers for my printer. Boy, if this isn't cheerful wedding weekend talk. Are you happy yet that you dragged it out of me?"

"Vernie, I'm sorry."

She shook her head, almost spilling her tea. "No. I'm just throwing a pity party. Can I get you a party hat?"

"Please! But would you hate me if I said it isn't that bad? You just finished saying the thing that makes a person interesting is that they're passionate about the things they love. You're the most passionate person I know."

Vernie smiled, but it was a weak one, especially for her.

"I know the answer to your problem," I said.

"Oh?" she said, lifting an eyebrow. "Well, please enlighten."

"We need to get you laid."

I sort of said this without thinking, but I immediately regretted it. I mean, Vernie was seventy-four years old.

But of course she howled. "Oh, you have no idea how right you are!"

I heard voices out on the porch—Otto and Gunnar back from the beach.

I pointed at Vernie. "We'll continue this conversation later," I said.

"No, I think I'll take option number two," she said. "I'm going to start doing a much better job of lying about my true feelings."

*   *   *

Later, after Nate and the others were back from the beach too, we all had lunch—deli salads and cold cuts—and I was starting to think that maybe the weekend had turned a corner. I still didn't know what was going on with Otto, but Vernie had perked up a bit (she probably would have said she was faking it better, but I had a feeling our little conversation had cheered her up).

Kevin seemed a lot more relaxed too, and I couldn't help feeling a little proud. I had officially cheered up two different people—Kevin and Vernie—in the space of thirty minutes.

Then Nate looked over at Kevin, took a big bite of his turkey sandwich wrap, and, talking with his mouth full, said, "So how long before you and Russel have kids? You used to yabber about that all the time back in school."

CHAPTER SEVEN

Everyone fell quiet, even as we kept eating—so quiet you could hear actual *swallowing*. All of my friends knew exactly how I felt about kids, and now they knew how Kevin felt too, so they could easily deduce that it had to be some kind of issue between us. Min already knew for a fact that it was.

Kevin reached for the cranberry quinoa salad. "Oh, that was a long time ago," he said to Nate. Then he immediately changed the subject. "My skin is still stinging in the places where the wetsuit didn't cover."

"I know!" Ruby said. "Me too."

"Rack off, mate, it wasn't *that* long ago," Nate said to Kevin. "Just a coupla years. Is it the whole gay thing? You used to tell me that didn't matter."

I couldn't help but wonder: Are all straight guys this clueless? Even Gunnar wasn't like this.

"*Dude*," Ruby said to Nate, "catch a clue."

Which just goes to show that while lesbians and straight guys might have similar brains, there are still some pretty big differences.

Nate's eyes danced from Kevin to me, then lingered, like he was finally putting two and two together.

"More potato salad?" Min said to the table. "It's made with pesto, right?"

I nodded yes even as everyone shook their heads no to the salad.

"Don't drink coffee," Nate said at last.

"What?" Ruby said.

"Before using a wetsuit. Or anything with caffeine. It shuts down the blood vessels, so it makes you feel colder."

After that, the conversation finally did move on—to the world's sixty zillionth conversation about whether Apple still deserves their reputation for innovation, I think. I wasn't really listening.

Later, when we were cleaning up, Kevin leaned in close to me and said, "That really was a long time ago when I told Nate those things. Seriously. I don't think that way now. It's not just you. I don't want kids any-more either."

I smiled and nodded. "I know. It's fine, really."

But a few minutes later, Min stepped up to me and said, "Hey, you want to go for a walk?"

And I hope it doesn't make me sound like a jerk that I said, "Yeah, let's go."

Inevitably, we found ourselves walking down the road to Amazing.

Min didn't say anything like, "Wow, that was rough back there, how are you doing?" And she didn't look at me all concerned either. Which was great, because it really wasn't a big deal. On the other hand, I knew that if I wanted to talk about it, she was more than willing to listen.

Instead, I said, "Are you mad at Gunnar?"

"For moving that orca?" she asked.

I nodded.

"Well," she said, "he committed a felony. But this is your wedding, and I believe him when he said he moved it farther down the beach. So I guess this is one of those times where you sort of turn the other way and pretend it didn't happen. Like when a friend tells you no one understands her like Taylor Swift."

I smiled. "How do you think he did it?"

But Min looked at me with this droll expression, and we both laughed. This was an ongoing joke between the two of us, how pointless it was to even *try* to understand the conundrum that was Gunnar.

"Ruby is no dummy either," I said, "is she?" I didn't want to talk about what Nate had said at lunch, but I could at least reference Ruby being smart enough to know what an idiot he was.

"Did you think she was?" Min said.

"No, but you know how it is. Everyone talks about emotional intelligence and 'different learning styles,' but who really believes in those things? It's not until you see them in action with people like Gunnar and Ruby."

"Actually, I think almost everyone else believes in those things. It's just us bookish, verbal types, people like you and me, who are skeptical. Because if there are different ways to be smart, it means we're not special."

"Well, hey," I said, "don't you think we brainy geeks should get *something*? We gave the world *Game of Thrones*, the Internet, and, you know, *science*. But still people laugh at us. Everyone says, 'We're all geeks now!' but it's so not true. The cool kids still run this world, same as always, and you damn well know it."

Min laughed.

"Are you worried about her spending so much time with Nate?" I asked.

"Ruby? You mean because they might run off together?" When I half-shrugged, Min laughed again, and said, "Oh, God, no! Ruby is the most lesbian lesbian I've ever met. They're just friends."

I nodded, and we kept walking down the road to Amazing. At this point, I felt pretty great. The wedding was back on track, that thing Nate said really was forgotten, and the air was crisp and clean. Even better, I was looking forward to seeing the ruins of Amazing again. What *had* happened to those people all those years ago? I was already spinning this fantasy about Min and me figuring it out. Yeah, I knew that people had been investigating this mystery for years, but so what? We'd be like Veronica Mars! Talk about Revenge of the Nerds: two geeky friends are staying on the island for a weekend wedding, and they stumble upon some clue hidden in the ferns, missed by all the investigators before. Or maybe it was simply a question of being smart enough to look at the ruins from a slightly different point of view, and our seeing what should have been obvious to everyone else, but had been missed because of all their stupid preconceptions.

Yes, this was all a silly fantasy—I wasn't serious about it, and it wasn't like I was going to mention it to Min, especially after she'd teased me earlier, saying the mystery of Amazing was exactly my kind of thing. But somehow it really did excite me.

We rounded the corner around the hill, and the little cove came into view.

Min and I weren't alone. A man walked toward us through the trees, up the trail from the water.

So much for my Veronica Mars fantasies, I thought.

It wasn't just that. I'd been starting to think of Amazing as a quiet little oasis from the world for Min and me, a place out of time. But that was silly too. It's not like other people didn't have a right to be here.

Min and I kept walking forward, until we all met at the end of the road.

He was older, in his sixties, but displayed Vashon Island's usual mix of contradictions: he was big and burly, but somehow soft and sensitive too. His face was craggy—like he'd spent a lot of his life outside doing something manly, maybe working on a fishing boat—but he had hoop earrings in both ears and a hipster-y man bun. He was wearing flannel and denim with thick boots, all weathered, but a beaded yin/yang symbol hung down from the zipper of his jacket.

"Howdy!" he said, friendly-goofy.

"Hello," Min said.

Then none of us said anything. I wanted to ask what he was doing here, but that felt a little territorial.

"We're staying at the Amazing Inn," I explained. "I'm getting married. I'm Russel, and this is Min."

"Well, congratulations to you both!" the man said.

"No," I said, "I'm not getting married to her." But I didn't tell him who I *was* getting married to, that it was a man named Kevin. Even after all these years, it felt weird to come out to people I didn't know, especially old people like this guy.

He nodded like what I'd said made sense. "I'm Walker," he said, giving one of those names where you're not sure if it's the first name or the last.

"You live here on the island?" Min asked.

"Sure do. Right over there." He made a gesture, but I couldn't see any houses through the trees.

"Christie—the woman we're renting from—told us all about this place," I said. I nodded to the ruins. "The town of Amazing? It's a pretty interesting story."

Walker took it all in, almost inhaling it. "Isn't it?"

That's when it occurred to me: maybe my little Veronica Mars investigation didn't have to end after all. Amateur detectives interviewed people, didn't they? And who knows? Maybe the people on the island would know secrets that off-islanders didn't.

"What do you think happened?" I asked.

"What?" he said.

"To the people of Amazing."

He laughed. "Well, that's the big question, isn't it?"

Min and I were quiet, listening. It felt like she was as interested as I was.

Walker eyed us. The fact that we seemed so genuinely interested was somehow making him take the mystery of Amazing more seriously too.

"Mass suicide," he said at last. "At least that's what I always heard."

Mass suicide? I thought. This wasn't a very cheery thought, especially on my wedding weekend. On the other hand, it made more sense than an alien abduction. And I had said I wanted to know the truth.

Min nodded. "That's what the articles all said."

I felt stupid. Min had mentioned that album of articles back at the house, but I hadn't even bothered to look at them. Some amateur sleuth I was.

"But Christie said people disappeared without a trace," I said. "So what about the bodies?"

He nodded toward the rocky promontory to the left of the cove, the one that looked out over the water. "They jumped. The water took them away."

105

Min and I stared at that outcropping of land, breathless. The sky was even darker now, but I made out a vague trail up the hill. It was sort of impossible not to visualize a line of people standing there, winding their way up to the top of the rock, and then, one by one, jumping out into the water. I imagined an old man with a cane and fur hat, and a woman with fly-away hair and an apron still covered with flour from the kitchen. A strapping young father stopped to clean his spectacles on his shirt, and another woman held the hands of two small twin boys (somehow the fact that it was twins made it especially tragic). Behind them, down the hill, the line of townsfolk twisted like the tail of a snake.

"But still," I said to Walker, "the *bodies*. Wouldn't they have washed up somewhere?"

"Maybe so," he said. He nodded out to the water again. "But that's Puget Sound out there, one of the narrowest parts. It doesn't look like it, but that water flows *fast*. If the tides were right, they coulda been all the way up to the San Juan Islands within an hour. Maybe some of them *did* wash up, but it was so far away that no one put two 'n two together. Or maybe they'd been in the water so long by then that no one recognized 'em."

I wasn't familiar enough with forensics, or Puget Sound, to know if what he was saying made any sense, but it didn't seem completely crazy. It was a century ago, when the whole area was still pretty remote, and communication was probably seriously lacking.

Still, it was pretty damn depressing. Part of me wanted to go back to the theory about alien abduction—the idea that the descendants of Amazing were still alive in a space ship somewhere, living on, unbeknownst to them, in some perfect recreation of their town.

"I guess the other question is why," I said. "Why would a whole town commit suicide? Was it some kind of—?" I looked at Min. "What was that famous cult back in the seventies, where everybody killed themselves by drinking poison Kool-Aid?"

"Jonestown," she said.

I looked at Walker, but he smiled.

"Well, if we knew that," he said, "we'd have already solved the mystery, wouldn't we?"

Fair enough, I thought.

"I'm curious," I said. "Is anybody still trying to figure out what really happened? Seriously investigating it, I mean?"

"Oh, you know how it is," Walker said. "Every few years someone comes out here and makes a big deal about starting up an investigation—some grad student or something. But it's all for show. After all these years, what is there left to find? Besides—" At this, he leaned in close. "Do we really *want* to solve it? Isn't it better that there's still a little mystery left in the world?"

Min and I both chuckled.

"Absolutely," I said.

"Well," Walker said, shuffling his feet a little, "congratulations to you and your—"

"Husband," I finished for him, and I felt a flash of pride. Just because it was awkward to come out to people I didn't know, that didn't mean I didn't ever do it.

His craggy face broke into a grin. "That so? Well, good for you!"

He gave us a final wave, then turned and headed off into the trees.

After he was gone, Min looked at me.

"What?" I said.

"You're totally thinking about the two of us going all Scooby Doo and being the ones who finally figure out the mystery of Amazing, aren't you?"

"*No!*" I said, seemingly outraged by the suggestion. I hesitated. "Actually, I was thinking Veronica Mars."

She laughed.

"I know we're not going to do it," I said. "But wouldn't it be great?"

Min turned toward the rocky promontory—the place where the citizens of Amazing possibly jumped to their deaths. Then she looked back at me, a twinkle in her eye.

"Really?" I said. "You really want to go up there?"

"Don't you?"

I wasn't sure what I wanted. But I didn't hesitate to follow when Min started down the trail, then up the promontory. It was steep enough for switchbacks, but there weren't any. Instead the trail just angled directly upward, over ferns and between rocks, and I used them as handholds. It wasn't rock-climbing exactly—or if it was, it was an easy grade—but it was a pretty steep hike. Because of the incline of the trail, our feet scraped away the leaves and even the top layer of the soil, revealing a wet, rich dirt that was a reddish brown color and smelled like some exotic spice.

If people really had jumped to their deaths from the top of this hill—a *huge* if—was this the trail they'd used to get there?

Min and I didn't say another word until we reached the top. Tufts of grass grew in a small patch, surrounded by trees and ferns and jagged boulders. From that spot, we could see that the drop-off was much steeper on the other side of the promontory—a ragged cliff that plunged sixty or seventy feet down to the water, which sloshed onto rocks below. There was no beach here.

Is this where the people jumped?

I stared out into the waters of Puget Sound, and it felt a little bit like I was standing in the frame of a movie. Walker had said that the current moved by fast here, and it's true that the water wasn't anything like it had been that morning—still and glistening. Now it roiled and churned. But I couldn't see a current either. Somehow it seemed like it was moving in all directions at once.

I felt bad that I wasn't sad, standing in a place where lots of people could have died—a little like when I felt guilty about not being more upset about that dead whale. But I *didn't* feel sad. On the contrary, I was exhilarated. For one thing, we didn't *know* that people had committed suicide here—it was probably only a stupid story, not much more likely than an alien abduction.

The wind blew in my hair, and a spray of cool mist washed over me, and suddenly it seemed so stupid, my worrying about getting married (not that I'd been *that* worried to begin with). Walker was right about Amazing—about the importance of mystery in the world. Marriage was another mystery, but then so was all of life. You couldn't predict the future about anything.

Sometimes you just have to make a leap of faith and hope that things turn out for the best, I thought.

We stood there watching the world a few minutes longer, breathing in the wind, neither of us saying a word.

Finally, Min said, "Well?" She meant, "Ready to go?"

I took a deep breath. Then I said, "Yeah, I'm ready."

At that exact moment, the clouds broke, and it started to rain. I knew it had been clouding over, but it hadn't looked especially like rain.

In less than a minute, the whole world collapsed into a downpour.

CHAPTER EIGHT

Min and I were drenched by the time we made it back to the house, even though it had only been a five-minute walk (and we'd been under the cover of trees the whole time).

After we dried off, we joined the others in the main room.

"It's really coming down," I said.

"It *is*," Vernie said, sitting in a chair by the window with her Kindle.

"D-four," Ruby said. She and Nate were playing Battleship at the dining room table.

"Miss," Nate said.

I looked around the room. I didn't know if it was the rain outside or what, but everyone exuded calmness. Min joined them, taking a seat and starting to read her phone.

Kevin stood watch by the glass door out to the deck, staring at the rain. I crossed over to him. Outside, the raindrops made little explosions against the wood.

"H-eight," Nate said, over at the table.

"Oh," Ruby said. "Hit."

"Really?" he said.

"Yeah."

"Ripper, you little!"

Ripper, you little? Nate's Australian slang made no sense whatsoever.

To Kevin, I said, "I still say weather forecasts are mostly quackery, but I guess they were right this one time."

He nodded, but didn't smile. He kept watching the rain.

"It'll be okay," I said. "We'll just move everything inside tomorrow. That was the whole point of getting this big house, remember? Having a back-up plan."

He nodded again, but still didn't look at me.

I put my hand on Kevin's arm. "Seriously. It'll all be okay."

He put on a bright face at last, but only for a second. Then he turned away, hypnotized by the rain.

"E-three," Ruby said.

"Miss," Nate said.

I joined the others. I didn't want to harsh the mellow of the room, so I sat down to do a little reading of my own. I remembered what Min had talked about back in Amazing—that photo album somewhere in the house with article clippings about the whole mystery. I was about to ask her where it was when I noticed Otto off in a corner reading his phone.

There was a strange expression on his face: totally engrossed, but also sad, like he was watching YouTube videos of kittens being kicked.

I almost said something, but then I remembered what he'd muttered at the farmers' market about his being on social media—implying it was a bad thing. Out of curiosity, I fired up my own phone and did a quick search on his name.

There were lots of great articles on him and his whole story: how he created a web series about his life as an actor with facial scars, and how it eventually got him cast on *Hammered*. There were also lots of photographs and videos of him attending premieres and charity events, always in designer clothes (he really did clean up well). That all made me smile.

But as I kept scanning, I saw things I'd never seen before, things he'd never posted on Facebook or Tumblr.

For one thing, there was sort of a backlash against the show. This surprised me at first. From my point of view, it seemed like the world couldn't ever get enough movies and TV shows about college kids getting drunk and having sex. But a lot of people didn't like *Hammered*, including a lot of critics, and of course they felt the need to trash it online. This exasperated me. My attitude about TV shows had always been that if you don't like something, don't watch it. (That said, a few shows, like *Girls*, were so ridiculously overrated that they might possibly *deserve* to be trashed.)

Anyway, I kept reading, and I discovered that a lot of people were upset over Otto's character too. This surprised me even more. A positive character with facial scars in a major TV show? Who wouldn't think this was a good thing?

Now I was annoyed. Were people just stupid or what?

Weirdly, even some other burn survivors were upset. I found one post in a disability forum, "Otto Digmore Should Be Ashamed of Himself!"

It read:

There's a new show on the CW, *Hammered*, which includes a burn survivor character by the name of Dustin, played by an actual burn survivor actor, Otto Digmore.

I guess I'm not surprised that Dustin is barely in the show at all. He's lucky if he has four lines per episode. I'm also not surprised the character is completely defined by his scars. At the same time, we don't really learn anything about him, about his treatment regimen, the pain he's in. He's always happy and cheerful. No scary emotions from the scarred guy! Naturally, he's completely asexual too, the one character in this whole stupid teen sexy comedy show who never gets laid.

But be careful what you wish for. In the "No One Wears Tighty-Whities" episode, Dustin finally gets his own storyline. In this Very Special Episode, it turns out people are making fun of him for being scarred! Of course he's completely powerless to solve his own problem. That's a job for our hero, Mike Hammer, whose heart finally grows three sizes that day, and he steps in and tells the bullies to go to hell. Basically, Dustin only exists so Mike can learn an Important Lesson About Tolerance, and the show can show us what a great, decent guy Mike is, in between all his debauchery and casual sex.

I'm not sure what pisses me off more about this show: the idea that it gives such a completely stereotypical view of burn survivors, or that the producers are making money off our pain.

FUCK YOU, CW!

And Otto Digmore, you should be ashamed of yourself!

Now I was completely confused. This didn't make any sense at all. Was it like how some LGBT people wrote about gay and trans issues online? No matter what anyone did, it wasn't enough. They assumed the worst possible motives about everyone except themselves, thinking the entire rest of the world was one hundred percent evil, completely consumed by racism, sexism, and transphobia (even when, I'm sorry to say, things were sometimes a lot more complicated than that).

I kept reading about Otto, and I saw things that downright shocked me, which is really saying something given that it was the Internet.

Someone had even posted pictures that were supposedly of Otto naked, from some hook-up website. I was pretty sure the photos weren't of him, but so what if they were? Who hasn't taken pictures of themselves naked? And let's face it: Otto's scars gave him a unique dating challenge. I'd been out with him to bars and clubs, and people always stared, but no one—not one single person in all the time I'd been out with him—had ever asked him to dance, or asked him out, or even come up to talk to him.

Not everything I read was bad. Some people wrote supportive stuff, and Otto had plenty of admiring fans: he was a good-looking guy, full stop, no qualifiers necessary, and his body seemed even better now than when we dated. At some point, Otto had posed for a series of sexy shirtless beefcake photos, which I thought was so incredibly cool, and probably the most subversive thing imaginable a guy like him could do. I was so proud that I lived in a time when a guy with a scar covering half his face and part of his body could be a sex symbol.

But I couldn't get over what other people were saying online—about how he was a freak, how it looked like his face was melting, and on and on. There were even a whole bunch of evil hashtags: #OttoDigmoreSkinCare, #OttoDigmoreIsOnFire, #ScarierThanOttosFace.

Seriously? I thought. Making fun of a guy who had scars on his face? Talk about punching down.

At this point, I was outright livid. I honestly couldn't remember the last time I'd been so angry about anything.

As I sat there stewing, Otto got up to use the bathroom. I followed him, waiting in the hallway outside until he was done.

When he came out again, I said, "*Fuck* them!"

He flinched. He hadn't expected me to be waiting for him.

"What?" he said.

"I did a search on you," I said. "I saw the kinds of things that people are writing."

"Russel—"

"No, seriously. Fuck them. Just *fuck them.*"

He sighed and slouched back against the wall. "It's not that easy," he said.

"Sure it is! Fuck them! Fuck them, fuck them, fuck them!"

Otto smiled, but it wasn't like he was really hearing me.

"I mean it!" I said. "Just fuck them all to hell."

He turned to look at me. "Did you see the Reddit stuff? Or the 'Otto Digmore' Halloween costumes?"

I shook my head no. Apparently, I hadn't even seen the worst of it!

"A year ago, I would have thought the same thing," he said, "that I could blow it all off, or even laugh about it. But it's different than you think. The hatred of the Internet is so strange. You can't imagine what it feels like until it's directed at you. It's like it has an actual substance, like it's a hurricane, dark and ugly and evil." He stopped and stood upright again. "Oh, God, listen to me. I'm sorry, Russel. I get a role on a sitcom, all my dreams come true, and here I am bitching about it to you."

"Otto, knock it off. I *asked* you. Of course you can talk about this stuff. Just because things are going well, that doesn't mean your life is perfect. I totally get how in some ways, it might even be worse."

He thought about it for a second, then he said, "Fame isn't what I thought it was going to be. I mean, some things are great—a *lot* of things are great. But still."

The truth is, it was weird talking to Otto about this. I would've given anything to be able to say things like, "Fame isn't what I thought it was going to be." Still, this was *Otto*, who was the most deserving person of fame in the whole world. I was jealous, but only a very little bit.

"So stop reading it," I said. "The stuff online. I know it's probably hard, but force yourself."

"That's what everyone says, but it's so much easier said than done. Seriously, I saw Jennifer Lawrence at this thing a couple of weeks ago?"

"You know Jennifer Lawrence?"

At least he had the decency to blush. "Ah, Russel, I really am sorry. Really? I'm name-dropping? How pathetic is that?"

"No! Are you kidding? You know Jennifer Lawrence! That's definitely okay to talk about!"

"I don't *know* her. I've *met* her. Like, twice. Anyway, one of those times we had a conversation for a whole ten minutes, and we talked about this."

"About how they stole her nude photos," I said, nodding. But I immediately felt like an idiot. Why in the world had I brought up nude photos?

"Not only that," Otto said. "All of it. How she was so beloved, and then the whole backlash, and the Sony email thing, and yeah, the nude photos. And also about the Internet in general, the idea that everyone has an opinion about you, and a lot of people have a really, really strong *negative* opinion. Anyway, it doesn't really matter if you read it or not, somehow you know it's there. Publicists and executives and show-runners, they talk about it. And then reporters ask you about it—they Google the hell out of you, and they just assume you've heard it all."

"I'm sorry," I said. "I didn't know any of that. And somehow you have to let it not bother you anyway. Wow, that really does sound hard." I thought about what to say. "Oh, hey, what was that great tweet by Gabourey Sidibe last year when people criticized her for looking fat in that dress? 'I cried about it all night on my private jet on my way to my dream job.'"

Otto nodded once, but didn't say anything.

"What?" I said.

He was conspicuously silent.

"You know Gabourey Sidibe too, don't you?" I said evenly.

"Well, I mean, I've *met* her. That's all!"

"Can I alter what I said a minute ago? Fuck *you*."

Otto smiled—his first genuine smile since we'd started talking.

"For the record," he went on, "celebrities always say that in public, that we're crying over insults all the way to the bank. And I mean, yeah, it's true. I live a good life. But the 'brave face' stuff is a lie too. All this crap people are throwing at me? It's still really, really hard."

"I bet."

He thought for a second, then he lowered his voice. "Someone even posted *my* nude photos."

So they were *of him?* Still, I pretended that I hadn't seen them. "Oh, man, Otto, that so sucks."

"Why do people do stuff like that? Seriously, I don't understand it." Now he sounded like he was going to cry.

"Because they're mean, ugly, small, petty people who've never done anything important or interesting or successful. And they come upon you, who *is* important and interesting and successful, and they can't stand it. It drives them crazy that you're everything that they're not. So they lash out. If you're happy and they're not, their solution is to try to make you as unhappy as possible too. Honestly, I think they're like the villain in some Dr. Seuss cartoon—it's exactly that straightforward. They're standing up on a mountain listening to you be joyful and happy, and they're absolutely seething, so they decide they have to dump all over you and be as ugly as possible. But it doesn't work. Oh, sure, they can make other people feel shitty about themselves for a minute or two—you and Gabourey Sidibe and *Jennifer fucking Lawrence*. But they can't make themselves feel any better. In the end, I think they feel even worse, because they know in their heart of hearts just how small and pathetic they really are."

119

When I was done, Otto didn't say anything for a second. Then his face broke into another grin. "Oh, my God, I think that was the best rant I've ever heard!"

"It's absolutely true!" I said. "Every word."

"You want to know what hurts me the most about the Internet? It's not the insults—people calling me waxface and freak. I'm used to that. I've heard that my whole damn life."

Now I was really intrigued. What was worse than somebody calling you a freak, than someone posting naked photos of you?

"It's other burn survivors," he said, slouching again. "It's all the criticism of the show, all these people saying that I'm hurting the cause. I'm, like, 'What the fuck?' Out of all people, they should understand. They should know how hard it is. They talk like I'm personally responsible for everything in the show, everything about my character. But I don't write the scripts! I'm a total nobody. And I signed a contract: I couldn't leave even if I wanted to, not unless I didn't mind being sued and never wanted to work in Hollywood again."

"You're right," I said. "It's totally unfair."

"And, I mean, it's not like the show is that bad. Is it? The writers did their best, but those first few weeks after we got picked up? It was *crazy*. The pressure was so intense. Besides, what about the good the show has done? What about the fact that the show cast me in the first place? I'm not trying to blow my own horn, but that's revolutionary. The producers took a *huge* chance, and they're really trying hard to do their best with the character. They deserve so much credit! So why aren't they getting any?"

"Because people are fucking assholes," I said. "See previous rant. Look, just because someone has scars, that doesn't mean they can't be jerks."

"But they're so *angry* about everything."

Otto was taking this all pretty seriously, so I decided to take it seriously too.

"Well, first of all," I said, "plenty of burn survivors *are* supporting you. Don't forget that, okay? It's only *some* people. Probably a really, really small percentage. I read things online all the time, and I think, 'I don't know anyone who thinks like that.' But people say something shocking and outrageous, and they get all the attention."

"I know, I know. Why is that so easy to forget? The praise barely even registers, but the criticism sticks with you until the day you die."

"As for the rest of it," I said, "well, I don't get it either. Then again, I've never understood that kind of stupid rage. How is shitting-all-over-everything a political strategy? I know that's easy for me to say— non-scarred, middle class, cis-gendered, white kid from the suburbs. But if you're going to get angry, it has to be anger with some kind of *point*. If it's just that stupid, no-perspective, lash-out-at-everything anger, not only does that not change things, I actually think it makes it worse."

Otto nodded.

"But you're not doing that," I said. "You're out there, putting yourself on the line and being real and making an actual difference. If you want the whole truth, I don't think I've ever been so proud to be friends with anyone in my life as I am with you."

Otto wiped his eyes—he was crying for real now (I was a little too). But he was also standing taller, definitely more confident.

Suddenly he hugged me, holding me tight. Despite not being a hugger, I squeezed him back just as hard.

"Thanks, Russel," he said. "That really helped."

"Anytime," I said.

He pulled back at last, wiped his eyes again, and said, "You know, that was almost as good as the advice Jennifer Lawrence gave me."

And I whacked him hard on the shoulder and said, "Fuck you!" and then, both of us laughing, we walked arm-in-arm back out into the main room.

I admit I hadn't expected to spend my wedding weekend making everyone else feel better about themselves, but I honestly didn't mind, because it was turning out that I was actually pretty good at it. I was kinda sorta impressed with myself. Anyway, I'd done my good deeds for the day, and now I could finally relax with the others.

I kept expecting the rain to let up, but it never did. It thrummed on the roof like the whole house was a vibrating bed. But this was fine with Gunnar, who was eager to show us all how the house's rain dispersal system worked in lieu of gutters. (Basically, the rain rolled down into these little trays that somehow sprayed the water out into the yard, all without any power source. I'd explain it more, except I didn't really listen.)

Before I knew it, it was time to eat again—an assortment of fried and baked chicken from the grocery store, along with baked tofu for Min, who was vegetarian.

Once we all sat down at the table to eat, I said, "How was it possible to get all this chicken for fifteen bucks? How is anyone making money on that?"

As soon as I said it, I regretted it. Saying something like this in front of Min was a little like throwing chum to a shark.

Sure enough, she said, "Because it's factory farmed. In 1920, a chicken cost a person two and a half hours of the average wage. Today, it costs fifteen minutes of wages. But it's only cheap because corporations don't pay the full cost of their product. The rest of us pay in the form of pollution, greenhouse gas emissions, and outright subsidies."

No one said anything for a second. As great as Min was, and as much as I admired her passion, she sometimes did have a way of killing a conversation.

"That doesn't even get into the question of how chickens are raised," she went on. "It's not what most people think."

Keep in mind that the rest of us were eating chicken when she said this. We all sort of hesitated, mid-bite. Alas, not only did Min sometimes kill the conversation, she didn't always know she was doing it.

Vernie dabbed her mouth with her napkin. Then she said, "I wish I'd known we were attending a lecture. I would have brought a pen to take notes."

There was another silence, this time an extremely awkward one. Chairs creaked. Min could definitely be a bit sanctimonious, and I'd sensed before that Vernie wasn't crazy about it, but I hadn't expected them to directly butt heads like this.

I felt like I should say something, but I had no idea what. I know I'd somehow taken it upon myself to make everyone feel better this weekend, but how could I possibly take sides between Vernie and Min?

Then Ruby said, "Oh, hey, we have some friends who keep chickens!" She touched Min on the hand. "Sarah and Meg?" Ruby turned back to the whole table. "Anyway, after all the money they spent on the coop, the feed, and the chickens—including the ones that were eaten by raccoons—they figured out what it cost them. Nine dollars an egg!"

The table laughed, more in relief than anything, and Min laughed too. I couldn't help but think: *This is interesting*. Ruby was managing Min's sanctimoniousness the way I'd been trying to manage Kevin's anxieties about the wedding. In this case, Ruby had tried to distract Min.

It worked, too. Gunnar started talking about raccoons—something about how, like crows, they're so much smarter than anyone thought. It didn't seem like there was any lingering bad blood between Vernie and Min, either.

And speaking of Kevin's anxieties, if he was still preoccupied, he was hiding it pretty well.

A few minutes later, Nate looked at Otto. "So what's it like?" he said. "Being famous and everything."

Otto wiped his fingers. "It's good," he said. "Well, I mean, it's great. It's funny though. Technically, my job is an actor, but sometimes it doesn't seem like I do a whole lot of that. Even after hair and make-up, I mostly just wait around for them to set up lights, and block the scenes, and do everyone else's close-ups first. And I also do a lot of promotion. Acting is, like, fifty percent waiting, forty percent promotion, and ten percent actual acting. But that sounds like I'm complaining, and I'm not."

Everyone nodded, even though, like me, they probably didn't have any idea what he was talking about.

"Sounds like a piece of piss," Nate said. "What's it like being on all the talk shows? Kevin said you were on *The Tonight Show*."

"*Stephen Colbert*," Otto said. "And I did *Seth Meyers* too. Honestly, I don't think I've ever been so nervous. At one point, the producer came to me in the green room and said, 'Have you taken your Xanax yet?' like it was just assumed I'd be on some kind of anti-anxiety drug. I wish I *had* been."

"You were great," I said. He had seemed a little nervous, at least on *Colbert*, but he'd also been modest and charming in a way that is absolutely impossible to fake.

"One guy said I looked like a deer in the headlights," Otto said.

That's when I realized that Otto probably didn't want to be talking about this—that it was yet another reminder of how people talked about him online.

"Anyone want more chicken?" I said.

"What the hell?" Vernie said, raising her plate. "I've always considered myself a moral monster."

So much for there not being any lingering resentment between Min and Vernie. And also so much for my spending the weekend solving everyone's problems.

Kevin's face darkened. Then he stood up to get more Squirt, even though his glass was still almost completely full.

This was too much. I could handle Vernie and Min butting heads, and maybe even Otto's discomfort, but I couldn't handle Kevin being disappointed with our wedding weekend. I'd promised him that everything was going to be okay.

"Oh, hey!" I said to Vernie. "I just thought of another single-location screenplay idea." I quickly explained to the table what that meant, the kind of ideas I'd been brainstorming lately. Then I said, "So how about a movie called *Green Room*? The story of this guy waiting to go on this late-night talk show."

"I wish that was interesting," Otto said, "but it's not. Waiting in a green room, I mean, not your idea."

"Yeah," I said, sinking lower in my seat. "Probably not."

"No, wait," Kevin said. "Say it's about a comedian. You know, the person who always goes on last? And the movie is about him and the other celebrities waiting in the green room."

I looked at him and smiled.

"Everyone's nervous," Kevin went on. "They're all sort of down on their luck, and they all need a break, so they're jockeying against each other, trying to undercut each other's confidence. Maybe there's an evil producer too, playing them off each other. One by one, they each go out onto the set of the talk show, and the comedian watches them on the monitor—and oh, hey, the only time we ever see the talk show host is on that monitor, we don't ever see him in real life."

"I like it!" I said. "And there aren't any windows, so the green room is totally claustrophobic. And there's no cellphone coverage either, and maybe he even gets lost on the way to the bathroom. The longer the comedian waits, the more trapped he feels, and the more he comes to realize how important it is that he does well— that this really is his last shot at success. So he's really, really desperate. Finally, the comedian's time comes, and he goes out onto the set, and he's completely nervous, but he ends up killing it! We finally see the host for real at last, and he even invites the comedian over to the chair by his desk."

I looked over at Vernie for her initial reaction.

She thought for a second, then said, "It's not terrible. As long as there isn't a final twist at the end where he's really been in hell all along, and the talk show host is Satan, and he has to keep repeating the same night over and over for all eternity."

I stared at Vernie, because that was almost exactly what I'd just been thinking.

"What?" she said. "Am I right?"

"No!" I said. But then I blushed and said, "I'd been thinking the talk show host was really, like, St. Peter, and the studio audience has been judging him to see if he deserves to go to heaven. And maybe the comedian walks out a glowing door at the end."

She smiled an all-knowing little smile. I felt stupid, but it didn't matter because the whole point of my screenplay idea had been to get the weekend back on track, and it seemed to have worked.

"Well, you're right," I said. "It's more interesting if it's metaphorical. We create our own heaven and hell—that kind of thing?"

Before Vernie could answer, Nate said, "You should write about this weekend."

I clutched a drumstick.

"You know?" he said. "A bunch of people in a house for a weekend wedding, and how things keep coming up? Will they or won't they get married?"

Kevin stood up to start clearing the dishes.

Really? I wanted to say to Nate. What the hell was *with* him? He was supposed to be Kevin's best friend! Was he really this clueless?

Frankly, now I was annoyed. I loved my friends, but this was my wedding weekend. I was starting to think Kevin had a point about everything going wrong.

"Let's all move into the front room," Gunnar said, and everyone else immediately agreed with him, including Vernie.

You know how you can sometimes sense when people are secretly eyeing each other—when everyone else knows something you don't? That's what was happening now.

What in the world? I thought.

It was funny. All through dinner, I'd felt like the only one who had a handle on all the things that were really going on—all the subtext. Suddenly it seemed like everyone there knew something I didn't.

Everyone except Kevin. He didn't seem to be in on this either. We exchanged curious glances. After all the pointless drama of earlier, I was extremely wary about what might be going on.

We all cleared the dishes (except for Nate, who had very conveniently disappeared), then gathered in the front room.

Gunnar hit a switch, knocking out the lights. Meanwhile, Min set this Bluetooth speaker on the coffee table, and punched a couple buttons on her phone. The speaker exploded with both music and this rainbow of shifting lights.

"What's going on?" I said.

"What do you *think*?" Gunnar said. "It's your bachelor party!"

Our what? I thought. Between the lights and the music, it really did suddenly feel like a party, even though there were only seven people in the room. It also helped that, except for Kevin, they were all grooving out to the music—even Vernie (surprisingly good).

"What did you guys plan?" Kevin said, but he was smiling when he said it. So much for our friends ruining our wedding weekend.

Nate appeared at last, from out of the hallway. He was wearing his green doctor scrubs, and he was dancing too.

No, not just dancing, I thought.

Nate, Kevin's annoying straight best friend, was doing a strip tease.

CHAPTER NINE

This was crazy! A bachelor party with Nate doing a striptease? But the music blared, and the lights flashed, and somehow Vernie and Ruby had already arranged two of the padded dining room chairs in the middle of the front room, and Min and Gunnar were pushing me and Kevin down onto them.

Then Nate took charge. He wasn't dancing, exactly—it was more of that straight-boy strut that isn't graceful, and it definitely isn't polished, but it's confident and cocky.

He stopped right in front of us, striking a sexy pose, then, in time with the music, he yanked open the front of his doctor scrubs, baring his chest and shoulders.

His pecs bulged, and the hair on his chest—dark blond—was surprisingly well-trimmed, especially for a straight guy. Did he manscape or had he only shaved for this little show of his? Had he rehearsed it? Exactly when had he agreed to do this striptease anyway? Our friends could have been planning this bachelor party for weeks. Needless to say, they were all laughing and totally cheering him on.

I also wondered: *Exactly how far is this "joke" striptease going to go?*

Kevin leaned over, closer to me, and said, "I had nothing to do with this, I swear!"

"Oh, I believe you," I said, laughing. "'Cause you know I'd totally dump you if you did!"

But here's the strange thing: neither of us looked at each other when we said this. We couldn't take our eyes off of Nate.

Remember when I met Nate, and at first I thought he was really hot? Then he said those annoying things, and I told you I didn't think he was hot anymore?

That might have been another little lie. I never really stopped thinking Nate was hot. I just thought he was kind of a jerk *in addition to* being hot.

Nate kept strutting around. He was camping it up, not taking the striptease seriously, but that didn't necessarily make things any less sexy. If anything, it might have made it even sexier, because I could sort of pretend it was all a joke even as I was watching his every little move.

Then, once again in time with the music, he tore the top of his scrubs completely off, throwing the whole thing to one side. He was shirtless now, revealing toned arms and a lean torso that tapered down toward the shapeless, crumpled paper-like material that made up the bottom half of his scrubs (but not so shapeless and crumpled that I couldn't make out the bulge of his ass).

Suddenly I was face to face with Nate's abs. The ridges and muscles reminded me of a kaleidoscope—everything twitching and shifting in sync. Nate was a doctor now—in residency, I think. Weren't they supposed to be so incredibly busy? If so, how could he possibly have time to body-sculpt his abs like this?

Somehow I hated and loved those abs at exactly the same time. They even sparkled with this little sheen of sweat.

"Oh, God, my *eyes*!" Kevin said. "Nate, you were my *roommate*!"

He ignored Kevin and kept strutting and/or dancing. Nate had *definitely* rehearsed this thing, at least a little.

On one hand, I agreed with Kevin: this was incredibly awkward. It was Kevin's best friend, and I had a very strict personal policy where I made a point not to lust after friends, or friends-of-friends, even when they were very hot.

On the other hand, Nate had an amazing body, lean and tan and toned. I may have briefly noted his body before, in that wetsuit especially. Now I was seeing more of him than I'd ever imagined I would, short of walking in on him in the shower.

Nate kept dancing, closer and closer, smiling seductively, but also doing that thing strippers do where they pretend they're ignoring you, even as they have to be aware that you're watching their every little movement. I noticed for the first time that he was barefoot, and somehow his feet were sexy too.

Outside the rain kept falling, heavier now, and I could hear it trickling down windows and splashing out in the yard, even over the music. That made me realize how Nate's striptease had made me start to sweat (not surprisingly), so it sort of seemed like the perspiration was coordinated with the water sounds, like it was trickling down my body.

Nate stopped, standing tall with his feet solidly planted, still wearing only the bottom of his doctor scrubs. He finally met my gaze, then Kevin's—greeting us both with this sly grin and half-nod.

Then, in one sudden flurry of movement, he bent over, yanking down the bottoms of his loose scrubs. He stepped out of them as effortlessly as if he was wading in a pond, then he simply tossed them to one side.

I literally held my breath, not certain what I would see next. I mean, it wasn't like he'd really be naked, right?

He stood upright again, and I saw he was wearing a green Speedo. (Most American guys didn't wear Speedos for bathing suits, but I guess they were still pretty common in Australia, so it made sense that Nate would have one.)

He wasn't naked, but the Speedo, well, let's just say it didn't leave a lot to the imagination. It also looked surprisingly, um, full.

"Right *on*!" Gunnar shouted, and Ruby, Min, Otto, and Vernie all whooped it up. Min and Gunnar clearly knew about Nate's striptease in advance, but he had to be taking it a lot more seriously than they expected. Somewhere along the way it had gone from campy fun to outright sexual.

Nate sauntered closer, not really dancing now, but languid, seductive. Was he going to give us a lap dances or what?

"I can't look," Kevin said, covering his eyes, and Nate laughed (and even his laugh was somehow Australian).

Nate straddled me. His bulging crotch was right below eye level, which was absolutely ridiculous. I could see the ridges and bulges of exactly what was packed in his Speedo, the position it was all in and everything.

I can actually feel the heat of his crotch, I thought.

133

Legs wide, he lowered himself down farther. He definitely *was* going to give us lap dances!

I was laughing—this was, after all, still a big joke. Or was it? That line was rapidly being blurred.

Outside, the rain still splashed, harder now, and my whole body was slick with perspiration.

Nate's ass pressed down against my lap—specifically against my crotch. I'd never had a lap dance before, especially one from a guy, and suddenly I was understanding what all the fuss was about. Needless to say, he'd long since given me a boner—basically, I had a railroad spike in the front of my pants. I mean, the only thing coming between my dick and Nate's ass was a couple of layers of clothing.

Nate kept grinding himself against my crotch, even as he started running his fingers through my hair. Every now and then, he lifted himself upright, and I felt the bulge of his Speedo graze against my stomach. There was even less material between him and me there. It was almost sensory overload!

The rain was still splashing outside, and I heard a sudden gush, like a clog had broken somewhere, maybe in the rain dispersal system, and all the water had rushed out, but in my mind, it sounded like something much naughtier.

Remember a couple of pages ago when I said I had a strict personal policy where I didn't lust after friends or friends-of-friends? You knew that was another lie, right?

I was nervous. The whole idea of this being a joke was now shot completely to hell. Nate absolutely had to know that he'd given me a boner—he had to *feel* it. If I didn't know any better, I'd say he was specifically aiming for it. But it still didn't quite compute. How the hell did a straight guy know how to give a lap dance to another guy anyway? And *why* would a straight guy give a lap dance to a gay guy, even at the gay guy's bachelor party? I'd been a teenager at a time when having a straight guy knowing you thought he was hot was a really bad thing.

But Nate wasn't horrified. On the contrary, he seemed to be enjoying the effect he was having on me. He wasn't necessarily turned on—trust me, I was close enough to the bulge in his Speedo that I knew his degree of arousal almost exactly (it was still jiggling and not yet twitching). But he had a sly, evil grin on his face, and I remembered that these days, a lot of straight guys loved the attention they got from gay guys. They *liked* the idea that they could be sex objects.

Just when I thought I couldn't take it anymore, Nate stood up again and stepped back. I wasn't sure what to do about the railroad spike in my pants, but I was pretty sure it was disguised by the crease in my jeans, and if I leaned forward to cover myself, that would only call attention to it.

Nate worked his way over to Kevin, dropping his hands around Kevin's head, running his fingers through his hair too, then sinking down onto his lap.

"Oh, God, I can't believe this is happening," Kevin muttered. "Someone please *kill me now*!"

But Nate kept at it, grinding and flopping his crotch against Kevin's stomach like he'd done to me. Everyone laughed and cheered.

Below Nate, Kevin shifted in his chair ever so slightly, and I knew Nate had given him a boner too. But that didn't stop Nate, who lowered himself all the way onto Kevin's lap.

Nate smirked, incredibly pleased with himself that he'd inspired the desired response in Kevin—that he'd basically conquered Kevin and me both.

But then Kevin flashed his own evil little grin.

As Nate writhed and grinded on his lap, he leaned forward and licked Nate's torso. It wasn't a little lick either—it was long and slow. His tongue was a creature with a mind of its own, slowly worming its way upward until it zeroed in on Nate's nipple.

Naturally, everyone went absolutely nuts for that.

"Oh, *my*!" Vernie said.

For a second, even Nate was taken aback, but he recovered nicely, pulling Kevin's face into his chest and grinding some more.

(And can I just say? Watching my fiancé-and-future-husband lick and nuzzle the sleek, neatly trimmed chest of his hot Australian friend was breathtakingly hot. I hadn't expected this—it hit me a little like a freight train—and I immediately thought, "I wonder what exactly *this* could mean for our future marriage.")

Finally, Nate pulled away, not quite as cocky-confident as he'd seemed before. I was farther from Nate's bulge now, so I no longer had an exact read on his degree of arousal, but I think he enjoyed those lap dances a bit more than he expected, especially after Kevin licked his chest. I guess this whole straight-guy-letting-gay-guys-openly-ogle-him thing was sort of new territory for everyone involved.

Nate kept dancing, a bit more frenetically now, maybe wrapping things up.

Meanwhile, all this continued to unsettle me. What did it all mean? What would it be like around Nate now?

Outside, the rain still fell, and something creaked, then snapped—probably a tree branch breaking in the torrent of water.

Something snapped inside my head too.

What's the big deal? I thought.

I said before that a line had been blurred, but had it really? It's not like Nate had gotten drunk and crawled into bed with Kevin and me. This was a *bachelor party.* The whole point was to be fun and carefree and, yes, even sexy on the night before your wedding.

It's possible—*possible!*—that I had a tendency to over-think things, especially things like hot boys in well-packed green Speedos grinding into my lap.

Nate kept dancing, back to his straight-boy strut, even hinting that he was going to pull down the whole Speedo too and giving us a flash of his pubes.

I wasn't nervous anymore. Now I was only having fun.

"Talk about doctors without borders!" I said, and the whole room laughed.

We all clapped and hooted a minute more, then Min finally lowered the music, and Nate took a bow, then turned to shimmy back into his doctor-scrubs.

Everyone applauded, and Vernie fanned herself, saying, "I haven't been this hot since menopause."

After that, we broke for snacks and drink refills. (I stayed seated, for obvious reasons, but somehow Kevin managed to stand.)

As everyone was complimenting Nate, Vernie slid up next to me. "I hate to say this," she said, "but that was another movie moment."

"You think?" I said.

"Oh, absolutely. Who would've guessed Nate had *that* in him?"

"You have a point."

"But mostly it was the expression on your face. That's what made it a movie moment."

I was about to protest, but I knew it was pointless. I was the one behind the terrified expression, and even I could tell it had probably been priceless.

Behind us, Otto called to the crowd. "Hey, we're not done yet! Everyone get back in here."

So, clutching snacks and drinks, everyone wandered back into the front room. Kevin joined me again, and I looked at him as if to say, "*Now* what?" but the fact is, we were both enjoying this.

With Kevin and me back in the two chairs in the middle of the room, Min punched up something else on her iPhone: cheesy game show music.

"Okay, it's time for the Been Together Off And On For Ten Years Now And Are Finally Getting Married Game!" Otto announced to the room. Then he added, "Also known as the Newlywed Game. How well do Kevin and Russel know each other? Tonight we'll find out!"

Kevin and I glanced at each other again. How well *did* we know each other?

Actually, I thought, *pretty damn well*. I wasn't worried.

Min cut the music, and Otto handed Kevin and me dry-erase boards and pens, and quickly explained the rules. He was only talking to a crowd of five people, but he was remarkably polished and confident. Which I guess made sense since he was a professional per-former.

Finally, Otto turned to us and, "Are you ready?"

Kevin smiled coolly. "We've got this *down*," he said, and I nodded.

"Well, now you're just challenging fate," Min said.

"Okay, first question," Otto said. "Let's start with an easy one." He read from a list on his phone. "Write down who each of you think the other would say is the hottest Disney prince."

"Hottest Disney Prince?" Ruby said, confused. "You mean, like, Aladdin?"

"Yes, but he's too geeky," I said.

"Wait," Ruby said. "Is this, like, a gay man thing?"

"Are you kidding?" Min said. "Animated Disney musicals and handsome princes? It's a total gay man thing."

"Just Disney?" Nate asked. "Not, say, Pixar?"

"Like who?" I said. "The old man from *Up*? The rat from *Ratatouille*? Pixar doesn't do sexy, at least not sexy men. Neither does Dreamworks."

"But Disney does?" Nate said, fascinated, and Kevin and I nodded at the same time.

"Totally," Otto said.

Kevin scribbled something onto his board, then looked at me expectantly. Everyone was staring at me now.

I had to think. I knew who *I* thought was the hottest Disney prince, but I had to consider who Kevin would pick.

"I can't believe this," Vernie said from the audience. "He procrastinates even when he's working with the medium of dry-erase! Boooo! Get with the game, Middlebrook!"

I smiled, then wrote something on the board.

"Okay," Otto said. "Russel first. Who did Kevin say you would say is the hottest Disney prince?"

"There's not even, like, a question," I said. "It's Prince Eric from *The Little Mermaid*. Have you guys seen those online photos where someone turned the animated characters into actual faces? They're all hot—well, except for the guys in *Frozen*, but that was sort of the whole point of *Frozen*, how the princesses didn't need a hot prince to be happy. But Prince Eric? He's the hottest."

Smiling smugly, Kevin flipped over his board, and it read, *Prince Eric.*

I grinned, and people clapped gamely. But honestly, it really was so obvious I don't know how much credit we deserved.

"I didn't even know the prince in *The Little Mermaid* had a *name*," Ruby said to no one in particular.

"Okay," Otto said to Kevin, "who did Russel say *you'd* say is the hottest Disney prince?"

"This is difficult," Kevin said, "because I did have this brief thing for the older brother from *Big Hero 6*."

"Tadashi?" Otto said. "But he's not a prince."

"True," Kevin said, "but it doesn't matter anyway, because in the end, I think he knew I'd say Flynn Rider from *Tangled*. Who *is* a prince by the end of the movie. And also a total hottie."

I flipped over my board. It read, *Flynn Rider.*

"Yes!" I said, fist-bumping Kevin. "We're two for two!"

Ruby looked at Min. "They've really given this 'prince' thing a lot of thought, haven't they?"

"I told you," Min said. "Gay guys are crazy. Russel once told me he had a thing for Danny Phantom in that old Nickelodeon cartoon."

Otto sighed dreamily. "It was all about the snark."

"See?" Min said, and Ruby rolled her eyes.

Outside, the rain picked up again, washing across the roof in waves. Obviously, the rain didn't remind me of perspiration (or something naughtier) anymore. But I was a little worried that it would be freaking Kevin out—that he'd be obsessing about flooding or something. I looked over at him, but he seemed to be keeping it together, smiling and casual, not even noticing the rain.

"Okay, next question," Otto said. "Write down the item of clothing of yours that your future husband most hates."

Kevin and I eyed each other skeptically. But honestly, this was another easy one.

We both scribbled something down.

"Russel?" Otto asked.

"His metallic blue hoodie," I said.

Kevin flipped his board. *Blue hoodie,* it read.

"Seriously, you guys need to see it," I said. "It's horrible. It looks like the shell of a beetle."

"It does *not,*" Kevin said, pretending to be wounded, but actually giving the audience exactly what it wanted.

"Kevin," Otto said, "what does Russel wear that drives you crazy?"

"He keeps wearing his socks even when they have holes in them."

I flipped the board. *White socks,* it said.

We did another fist-bump. The fact is, we were *killing* in this game. We really did know each other well.

That was a good thing, right? On the other hand, I couldn't help but think: If we knew each other so well, did that mean our marriage was going to be boring? Walker, the old man Min and I met in Amazing, had said the world needed more mystery. Well, didn't marriages need mystery too, at least to stay interesting? If I was being neurotic about this whole "wedding" thing, this game might have caused me to start seriously pondering this. But I *wasn't* being neurotic, as I've already told you, so this was really more of a fleeting thought.

Otto started to ask another question. "A meteor is heading right for your house..."

"Ask something dirty!" Ruby called.

"Really?" Otto said. "Two questions in and we're already moving on to sex?"

"The first question was about Disney cartoons, but they managed to turn *that* into sex," Nate said.

"Said the guy who was just dancing around in his Speedo," Kevin said.

Everyone laughed, and it was all pretty funny, but it did occur to me—another totally passing thought!— that Kevin's and my relationship was so predictable it wasn't even keeping our best friends entertained.

"Okay, okay," Otto said to the group, "the pervy public has spoken." He scanned his list. "Here we go!" He turned to Kevin and me. "What is the naughtiest place the two of you have ever made whoopie?" He looked out at the audience. "That's how they put it on the Newlywed Game, right? They say 'making whoopie' rather than 'fucking'?"

Everyone laughed again while Kevin and I wrote our answers on the dry-erase boards.

"Kevin?" Otto asked. "What did Russel say?"

"The picnic gazebo," he said.

I flipped my board, and it read, *Stinky picnic gazebo.*

"Russel?" Otto said.

"The stinky picnic gazebo," I said, and Kevin flipped his board so it read, *Picnic gazebo.*

"Public sex?" Vernie said. "I'm *shocked.*" She turned to Min, sitting next to her. "We can only hope it was at night."

"Yeah," I said, blushing. "It always was."

"'Always'?" Ruby said. "You mean it was more than once?"

"It was back in high school!" I said. "Where else were we supposed to go?"

Kevin looked at me. "Actually...."

I thought about it. "Oh, right." I looked sheepishly out at the audience. "We may have been there *since* school too. It's complicated."

Everyone howled. I was starting to see why the show made a point to ask questions about sex: even when the couple knows everything about each other, like Kevin and I did, it could still be pretty entertaining.

"Thinking about your partner's total number of sex partners," Otto went on, reading from his phone, "are we talking single digits? Double digits? Or—God forbid!—triple digits?"

Kevin and I both made a point to blush and shift around awkwardly in our seats, then we turned to the dry-erase boards.

But honestly, I knew the answer to this too. I wrote down my answer on my board.

"So, Kevin," Otto said. "Single digits, double digits, or have you hit a triple?"

"Hmm," he said, then he made a big show out of counting it out on his fingers, making it seem like it was going on and on and on, and when people realized what he was doing, he got a good laugh.

"Single digits," he said at last. "Six guys and three girls."

"Three *girls*?" Nate said. "Is this why I had such a hard time getting dates when I was living with you in college? Bloody hell! You were cock-blocking me?"

"They were all back in high school," I pointed out, holding up my board.

Single digits, it read.

"And you *never* had a hard time getting dates in college," Kevin said to Nate.

"And Russel," Otto said, "what about you? Single, double, or triple?"

"What?" I said.

People laughed like I was making a joke, but I wasn't. I'd honestly forgotten that I had to answer the question too.

Here's the deal. Kevin was an extremely sexy man, but he was also a date-before-sex, one-on-one kinda guy. Which, frankly, was part of what made him so sexy: when you were with him, he made you feel that he *was* really with you, that it was all *about* you. Not like you were just a body, or another conquest, or a notch on his nightstand. So it was no surprise to me that he'd only ever been with five other people (the three girls didn't really count, because he'd been closeted and had only been doing it for appearances).

As for me, well, I was a one-on-one kinda guy too, and I've already said how Kevin and I were mono-gamous. But Kevin and I had been on-again-off-again for ten years. Which meant that there was plenty of time in there when the two of us were "off." In that time, I'd had a series of pointless relationships, and I may have fired up a hookup app once or twice (or a few more times than that).

The point is, I wasn't in the single digits anymore. (It's not like I was in the triple digits either! Basically, I was in the low double digits. Exactly *how* low is none of your damn business.)

"Double," I said to the gathering.

There was a moment's hesitation. Outside, the rain pitter-pattered, and something in the woods creaked.

Then everyone started oohing and ahhing.

"*Russel!*" Min said, but I had a feeling she was faking it. I used to live with Min and she was no dummy. She had to know the truth about my sex life.

Anyway, I had officially shocked my friends—and hopefully Kevin too. Truthfully, I was kind of happy that I still had some mystery. Maybe that meant our marriage would be an exciting one after all.

Then Kevin flipped over his dry-erase board.

Double digits, it said.

I stared at him, a bit dumbfounded. "How—?"

He grinned like someone stoned. "Seriously? You think you have secrets from me?"

I'd thought I did! And, honestly, I'd sort of *hoped* I did. What did it mean that I didn't?

"Next question!" Otto said. "It's fifty years from now, and of course you guys are still married. Are you Fit and Fabulous? Dirty Old Men? Or Get Off My Lawn?"

Kevin immediately started writing on his board, but I hesitated. How *did* Kevin see us in fifty years? It was Fit and Fabulous, right? Or maybe Dirty Old Men—in a let's-reclaim-the-slut-shaming-and-sex-negative-terminology kind of way.

But what if it wasn't? And no matter what he thought, what would we actually be? What if we did end up as two grumpy old men? Making whoopie—er, fucking—at the Stinky Picnic Gazebo had been pretty naughty, but was that the naughtiest thing we were ever going to do?

My eyes met Min's, and she sort of scowled at me, like she knew I was thinking about the conversation we'd had before, my worrying about growing older and becoming boring. She had a point: this was a stupid train of thought, even for me. And—maybe, just maybe—it was an outright neurotic one. It was a silly question in a stupid Bachelor Party game, made all the more stupid by the fact that, only minutes before, I'd literally been totally turned on watching my future husband lick sweat off his shirtless straight best friend's torso. Why would I think that Kevin's and my sex life would ever turn dull?

Then again, maybe it wasn't necessarily Kevin I was worried about making our life boring. Maybe it was me.

I'm definitely over-thinking things again, I thought, *like with the striptease.* But I should point out (again) that these were fleeting thoughts, barely worth mentioning

I uncapped my dry-erase pen, and sat poised to start writing.

But before I could write a single letter, the lights flickered once, then went completely dark.

"Oh, no," Kevin said, and I could already hear a note of panic in his voice. "I think the rain just knocked the power out."

CHAPTER TEN

"We don't know it was the power," I said, sitting there in the darkness of that house. "Maybe we just blew a fuse."

"No," Gunnar said as I heard him moving around in the shadows. "It's out all over the house." He walked to the window and looked outside. "I don't see any lights at all. Yeah, I think the power's out."

"An isolated house in the woods and the power goes out?" Vernie said. "That's never good."

"What do you mean?" Kevin said.

"Oh, I'm just kidding," she said. "I meant like in the movies. I'm sure it's fine."

"Yeah," Gunnar said, "it's probably just a line down somewhere." This was funny, though, because the rain now sounded like it had died down a bit, like the fever outside had broken. Still, with all the trees, power lines probably went down all the time on Vashon Island.

"But what do we *do*?" Kevin said. "Are we supposed to just sit here?"

The panic in his voice was more obvious now. Which made sense: he was thinking about the wedding tomorrow. It was one thing to move the ceremony

147

inside because of the rain. If there was still no power by then, could we hold the wedding at all? It would be a challenge for the caterers, that's for sure. And I had a vague memory of Christie saying something about how the house was on a well. Didn't you need electricity to draw water from a well?

"They'll get it fixed," I said. "The wedding's not for another sixteen hours."

"How can you be so sure?" Kevin said. "Things are different on the island. And we're not even on the populated part of the island."

No one said anything. The fact is, Kevin had a point. Growing up in the Seattle area, I'd been reading all my life about people in the rural areas who lost their power and didn't get it turned back on for days or weeks.

One by one, my friends switched on their phones, adding light to the room—soft, colorful glows.

I shuffled closer to Kevin and laid my hand on his back. "It's going to be okay," I said. "I'm sure they'll get the power back on in time."

Even now, I was determined to keep reassuring him. But Kevin was sweaty, and it wasn't from Nate's striptease anymore. He was so anxious the tension pulsed off his body.

If reassuring him wasn't working, maybe I could try to distract him, the way Ruby had distracted Min at dinner.

I looked around the room. "I see candles. Let's see if we can find some matches."

"I'm on it," Ruby said, heading to the kitchen where she fumbled through some drawers. "Got 'em," she said a second later.

She returned and started going around the room, carefully lighting all the candles and kerosene lamps.

We all watched her in silence, like it was some kind of ritual in church, the preparation for some ceremony. Now it sounded like the rain outside had stopped completely, the only sound being water dripping from the gutters—er, rain dispersal system. I guess the weather gods had accepted the sacrifice of the island's power grid, and they were satisfied for the time being.

Ruby kept lighting candles and lamps—there were a lot more of them than I would have guessed. Most of the candles were at least partially burned down. I hadn't noticed any of this before—some detective I was!—but now I realized that probably meant they had a lot of power outages at the Amazing Inn. In terms of the wedding, I couldn't decide if all those candles were a good thing or a bad one.

While Ruby lit the candles, I moved Kevin's and my padded chairs back to the dining room table.

Finally, the whole room was lit. It throbbed with light, all of it flickering and glowing. It was vibrant, but not bright, and the burning wicks hissed ever so slightly. It felt a little like we were all in the middle of a neon sign.

Still, no one said anything. We all sat down again, positioning ourselves in chairs and on couches so we were more or less in a circle.

It was funny: we could have easily kept going with the bachelor party, with whatever else our friends had planned. The fact that the power was out didn't really change anything. We'd turned down the lights before for Nate's striptease, and Min's party-light music speaker had a battery, so we could turn that on again if we wanted.

But the vibe in the room had changed into something different—more subdued, more sober. Somehow

149

the bachelor party part of the evening was over, and we all knew it, but that wasn't necessarily a bad thing. It was a prelude to something else, only the first course of a gourmet dinner. The difference is, I don't think anyone, not even Min and Gunnar, knew what came next.

"That was really fun before," I said at last, meaning the bachelor party. "We really appreciate it."

Kevin looked up. "Yeah," he said. "Totally unexpected."

"Although I'm disappointed we didn't play Pin the Cock on the Jock," I added.

The second the words were out of my mouth, I remembered the room included a seventy-four year-old woman, Vernie. But of course she laughed harder at my joke than anyone else, and I reminded myself that I needed to stop worrying about her, that she could more than hold her own in this crowd.

"It was Gunnar's idea," Otto said.

This made me smile, the idea of Gunnar planning all this. He'd also managed to use the party to diffuse the tension at dinner earlier—something that had been beyond me.

"No," he said. "Everyone helped. We did it via email."

In the silence that followed, the candles hissed and the rain dispersal system trickled.

Talk about a different vibe, I thought. I glanced over at Kevin, but he still looked anxious, worried about the wedding.

"I wasn't sure I wanted to come this weekend," Ruby said quietly. "I didn't know what it was going to be like. I don't know anyone except for Min. And this is someone's *wedding* weekend. I didn't want to intrude."

"Well, we're glad you did," I said. "Really glad."

"Me too," Ruby said. She took a sip from her beer bottle. "It's hard for me, being around people I don't know."

"Don't take this the wrong way," I said, "but that surprises me. You seem like one of the most confident people I've ever met."

She smiled. "That's what everyone thinks. But I was always the shyest kid in my class. I hated recess so bad, because you had to talk to people. I hated lunch, because you had to find a table to sit at. Whenever we had to give a presentation in class, I got so sick I couldn't go to school. At the end of the eighth grade, the class did one of those end of the year lists, where the whole class votes: Most Likely to Succeed, Cutest Smile, Best-Looking, things like that. It was the eighth grade, so the teacher said there had to be enough categories for everyone—everyone had to be picked for *something*. One of the categories was Shyest Girl, and I remember thinking how unfair that was. All the other categories were something positive—Best Personality, Best Dressed. But being shy wasn't positive, and it was the *only* category that wasn't something positive. Anyway, everyone voted, and the end of the year came, and they passed out the list, and there I was, expecting and dreading that I'd be named the Shyest Girl in class."

"And?" Min asked.

"They forgot me completely!" Ruby said. "They'd voted Marguerite Dunn as Shyest Girl. I was so shy that people didn't even remember I was there! I didn't say anything, and the teacher never noticed either."

Min reached over and took Ruby's hand, holding it tight.

"At one point, my parents brought me to a psychologist," Ruby went on. "She said I had extreme social anxiety. They tried therapy and medication and hypnosis, but nothing worked. The worst part was I could tell how disappointed my parents were. They weren't these big social butterflies—none of my family was—but they had no idea what to do with me, which made me feel even worse, made it all even more of a clusterfuck."

"What changed?" Vernie asked.

"One day when I was about fifteen, I woke up, and I just felt...different. I was tired of being invisible. It wasn't a conscious decision, like I woke up and said, 'From this point on, people will not ignore me! I will never get anxious in crowds again!' It was more like something in my brain had changed. I think it did. I went to school that day, and I felt like a different person. I looked people in the eye, I talked to them. And the thing about being so shy before, so invisible, was that it was almost like I was a new student. People had ignored me so much that they didn't really have an opinion of me. So when I started talking to people, it was like a fresh start. And in a couple of months, I had a whole circle of friends."

"Fascinating," Vernie said. "And you never felt shy or anxious again?"

"No," Ruby said. "It wasn't like that. I definitely get nervous. I still don't like parties, and I almost never go out to clubs or bars. But it feels more 'normal' now. Honestly, when I think back on myself, it really does seem like I was a different person. I don't judge her though, and I don't judge other people like that. I've never thought, 'She was so stupid, she wasted all that time!' She did the best she could. I feel sad for her more than anything. Like I said, it doesn't feel like I made a choice or did anything at all. I woke up one day feeling different. I guess that's the other thing that's sort of interesting. After a few weeks, I didn't worry that I'd turn back into that other girl, and I still don't, because like I said, it doesn't feel like it was me. It feels like someone else."

We all fell silent. It was a pretty great story, but I wasn't sure what to make of it.

Finally, Vernie said, "I wasn't sure I wanted to come either. I didn't think I'd fit in."

Part of me wanted to object, to say, "Vernie! Of course you would!" But something kept me quiet. It seemed like the evening had entered its Total Honesty phase, so I decided to let her talk.

"It really stinks getting old," she went on. "But sometimes I think the aches and pains, the physical stuff, are the least of it. It's the way people treat you. Or maybe it's not that at all—maybe it's the way you start to see yourself. Like most of your life is over. Which it is. You ask yourself, 'Are the *best* parts over? Have I already done the most important and interesting things I'm ever going to do?' And you can lie to yourself and say, 'No! Jessica Tandy won an Oscar when she was eighty years old!' Or you can be honest with yourself and admit that, yeah, the best part probably *is* in the past."

Now I wanted to reach over and take Vernie's hand, the way Min had done with Ruby. But she wasn't sitting next to me and I didn't want to make too big a show of it.

"I met my husband at a friend's wedding," Vernie said. "I was twenty-two years old. He was a friend of a friend of a friend, and I thought he was so handsome.

153

We talked and laughed, and he lit a match from a box of matches using only one hand. The wedding ended, but the night did not. We went out drinking and dancing, and we broke into the Japanese garden and drew our names in the sand, but the night still wasn't over. It wasn't the first time I'd had sex, but it felt like the first time I'd *chosen* to have sex. I felt like a woman for the first time in my life—no, I felt like Wonder Woman, strong and beautiful and invulnerable, like there was nothing in the universe that could stop me." She looked at Ruby. "It was a little like what you said. I went to bed one person and I woke up someone else, someone I liked a lot better than the person who had gone to bed."

We all nodded, but no one smiled a knowing or dreamy smile. It was something about the bittersweet note in Vernie's voice. We knew something bad was coming.

"I got pregnant, of course," Vernie said. "From that very first night. And Fritz and I got married, after knowing each other all of three months. I knew in my heart it was a terrible idea, but everyone told me it was the right thing to do—that it was all my fault to begin with, and it was the best thing I could do for the child. But it *was* a terrible idea. Fritz and I were nothing alike. The only thing we really shared was that single night—and a desperate loneliness and a feeling of wanting more. I didn't feel like Wonder Woman after that. I felt trapped and angry and resentful, not just at Fritz, but at the whole universe, one that had played such a cruel trick on me, making me feel so good, giving me a taste of freedom, then snatching the goblet away again."

We all listened to Vernie's story, breathless.

"I was depressed for years," Vernie went on. "Forget feeling like Wonder Woman, I didn't even feel like a woman, like a person. I felt like a cloud of dust wafting around the house, only visible in the sunlight. But then I found something that changed everything."

"Writing," I said.

Vernie nodded. "It saved my life. Writing finally made me a person again, it made me whole. It also ruined the lives of my children, but that's a whole other story. Anyway, this is all another reason why I didn't want to come this weekend. When I think of weddings, I think of that wedding where Fritz and I met all those years ago, and then our own pathetic wedding a few months later. To tell the truth, I haven't been to a wedding in more than thirty years. Can you believe it? But I'm so glad I came to this one. Because now I finally get to see how weddings can really be, what they're really all about. So I guess I was wrong before when I said that the best was all behind me. Because this is one of the best weekends of my life."

Yup, there was a lump in my throat. But I didn't go over to hug her or anything, and it wasn't just because I'm not a hugger. Somehow I didn't want to disturb the moment.

All I said was, "Thanks, Vernie."

I looked over at Kevin, but the shadows from the candles were weird, and I couldn't get a good read on his face, whether all these stories had distracted him from worrying about the wedding.

"I want to get married," Otto said quietly. "One day, I mean."

Once again everyone stopped rustling in their chairs, listening. I liked this, all our friends together, telling their stories—their *real* stories, not the bullshit ones we tell to make ourselves and everyone else feel better.

"I used to think I'd never meet anyone," Otto said. "But recently I met this guy."

"*What?*" I said, sitting upright in my seat. "And you're just telling me this *now?*"

Everyone laughed, and I was glad I'd read the moment right—that the room needed a little livening up.

"We only started dating," Otto said. "Like, three weeks ago. We're not even 'dating.' We've met up three times. That's why I didn't say anything."

"Where did you meet him?" Kevin asked.

"Well, Zachary Quinto set me up on this blind date," he said.

The room was quiet, but somehow the silence bulged like a balloon.

"You got set up on a date by *Zachary Quinto?*" I said. Before Otto could say anything, I cut him off. "Yeah, yeah, you barely know him!"

"Actually, I know Zachary Quinto pretty well. We did this charity event together this summer, and we ended up spending almost the whole day together. He's a really nice person."

"I'm sure he is!" I said.

"Tell us about this guy," Min said.

Otto thought for a second. "I didn't want to go out on the date. I mean, a blind date? Me? Are you kidding? But Zachary talked me into it."

"I'm sure he *did*," I muttered.

"Anyway, we met at the restaurant, and he seemed really great. He didn't stare at me, or act weird or anything, and I thought, 'Okay, maybe I was wrong, and Zachary Quinto was right.' We got our table and got to talking. And then he proceeded to reveal that he was a raging asshole. Stupid, bitchy, racist—the whole gay trifecta."

We all laughed.

"So what happened?" Min said.

"The waiter overheard our date, what a jerk this guy was," Otto said, "and as I was leaving the restaurant, he gave me his number."

"Sounds like the plot to a romantic comedy," Vernie said.

"It does. Anyway, I met him for drinks the next day. It turns out he'd recognized me from my show."

"Is that bad?" Min asked.

"Well, there's always a question: does this person want to be with me because I'm on TV? I know how that sounds, but for me, it's a lot like how it used to be. I always used to wonder if guys were going out with me out of pity. Now I wonder if they're going out with me because I'm on TV. Not that I really have time to go out anyway. This is, like, the first time I've gone out with a guy since the show debuted."

"Well, sure," I said, "because you're too busy going out with Jennifer Lawrence and Zachary Quinto!"

Otto and everyone laughed, and I was glad, because I was worried I'd finally pushed the joke too far.

"Right before I left to come up here, Spencer and I—that's his name, Spencer—were hanging out, sitting on his couch watching TV, and a bee flew by inside the house. We sat upright, panicking a little, both of us scared about getting stung. We knew we needed to get rid of it, but then we both said at exactly the same time, 'But don't kill it!' And we looked at each other, and there was this moment, you know? This connection. I thought, 'This is the kind of gentle, open-hearted guy I could spend my whole life with. He's exactly the opposite of that asshole Zachary Quinto set me up with.' Oh, and by the way? Zachary Quinto apologized for setting me up with that other guy. He was a friend of a friend, but he didn't know him as well as he thought he did."

"That's so sweet," I said. "Bonding over bees."

"Honey bee or wasp?" Ruby asked.

"Bumblebee, actually," Otto said. "But it would have been the same even if it *had* been a wasp. Circle of life and all that."

"Oh, the world always needs bees," I said. I knew Gunnar was crazy for bees, so I looked around the room for him. "Isn't that right, Gunnar?"

No one said anything.

"Gunnar?" I said, still searching.

He wasn't there.

"Where's Gunnar?" I asked the group.

"Must be in the bathroom," Kevin said.

I didn't remember Gunnar leaving the room. I thought back: when was the last time he'd said anything? I remembered him saying that it wasn't just him who had planned the bachelor party, that everyone had helped. Had he snuck out after that?

Knowing Gunnar, he was probably out collecting slugs.

After a few seconds of silence, Nate said, "This is quite a chinwag. Not like any buck's night I've ever been to."

"I don't know what any of that means," Kevin said. "And keep in mind that I lived with you for three years."

Nate laughed. "A chinwag is a conversation. And a buck's night is what we call a bachelor party Down Under."

"You do that on purpose, don't you?" Kevin said. "All that slang? You think you're being charming."

Nate preened for the camera. "But admit it—it works." He was quiet for another second, then he said, "I got my heart broken, right before I came here."

Nate had a story to tell too? This surprised me a bit.

"Mia?" Kevin said, and Nate nodded.

"Well," Nate said, "I guess I should tell the whole story. I actually met her at the pool, swimming laps. And there's something about meeting someone in your budgie smuggler." He looked at Kevin. "My *Speedo*. Happy?"

"Somewhat," Kevin said.

"It doesn't leave a lot to the imagination," Nate said, "which I guess you guys already know."

"I'll say," Vernie muttered, and everyone laughed.

"Anyway, it was interesting, seeing her in her swim suit," Nate said, "and having her see me, knowing how we look almost naked, but not knowing anything else about each other. I didn't even know if she was single, or straight, but one day I took a chance and asked her out. And she said yes. We met at the restaurant, and at first we didn't even recognize each other in clothes and with dry hair. We stood in a crowded lobby together for at least two minutes before we realized who we were. It was almost like we'd been expecting each other to show up for the date in our swim suits."

Not the worst idea I've ever heard, I thought.

"We talked for hours," Nate said, "and I thought it went great. So I ask her out on a second date, and once again she says yes. Then I keep asking, and she keeps saying yes until finally we are definitely 'dating.' Then one night I say, 'I love you.' And she immediately says, 'I love you too.' So I think we're in love, and for six months, we do all the things people do when they're in love. Then I ask her, 'Do you want to move in with me?' And she says, 'Yeah.' So she does. And I'm thinking everything is great.

"Then one day she comes to me and says, 'I'm not happy. I think we should take a breather.' And I ask her, 'Do you still love me?' And she says, 'I'm not sure, that's what I need to find out.' I was completely gutted, exactly like a fish. But a couple of days later, I ask her, 'Did you *ever* love me?' and she says, 'Of course I did.' That's when I looked back on our relationship, and I realized that at every point where someone asked a question, I was the one doing the asking, and she was the one saying yes. So I don't think she ever did—love me, I mean.

"At first I felt pretty stupid about that, that I hadn't seen it. And I was mad at her too, for not being honest. But then I realized that it wasn't necessarily us, it was the whole system that was screwed up. The guy is *supposed* to ask the girl out. If *she* does it, some people think there's something wrong. And he's supposed to be the first person to say 'I love you,' and all the rest. That's what's so screwed up about the whole thing. How could I have known? It was all perfectly normal, but it means people aren't honest about what they want, about what they really feel. If it hadn't been for that stupid script in our heads, maybe I would have sensed her hesitation, or maybe she would have been more honest with me."

He fell silent, and once again no one said anything.

There was a "poor little rich kid" quality to Nate's story, but it was still kind of touching. Then there was the *actual* touching that Nate had done during his strip-tease, all in the name of our bachelor party. Taken all together, I was starting to think that maybe I'd misjudged him—that he was a pretty decent guy after all.

I turned to Kevin, who looked like he was about to say something to the group, to reveal his great truth. I was glad, because I was still curious what he was thinking, if I'd distracted him from being worried about the wedding tomorrow.

Suddenly the lights flickered and came back on.

"*Whoa*," Ruby said, surprised.

It was definitely disorienting, like someone unexpectedly yanking a blanket off your head. It also felt awkward after the intimacy of the last few minutes, seeing everyone in the clear light again.

People shifted in their seats, and Nate stood up to stretch. The vibe of the evening was changing yet again.

A second later, Gunnar rejoined the group.

"Gunnar!" I said. "Where were you? Look, the power's back on."

"Not the power," he said. "That's still out. This is the generator."

"The house has a generator?" I didn't remember Christie saying anything about this either. Clearly, that house walk-through we'd done with her had been for shit.

Gunnar nodded.

"How did you know?" I asked.

"I didn't," he said. "But I looked around and I found one outside. There's plenty of propane too. We're good for the whole weekend."

"But how did you know how to—? No, wait, never mind." This *was* Gunnar, after all.

Gunnar looked over at Kevin. "I figured you'd want power for the wedding, right?" he said. "Even if the power comes back on, I didn't want you guys worrying about it."

Kevin stared at him, and even now I couldn't quite tell what he was thinking.

"Besides," Gunnar went on, "I told you before. It's my wedding gift to you. I'm making sure nothing gets in the way of your wedding."

"Thanks, Gunnar," Kevin said, nodding deeply.

"Yeah, thanks," I said, feeling a bit stupid about the mean-ish things I'd been thinking about him before.

After that, everyone wandered back to the kitchen for more food and drinks, and I happened to notice the dry-erase boards sitting on the floor, including the one Kevin had been using.

I couldn't resist flipping it over to see what he'd written about what he thought we were going to be like in fifty years.

Of course it was blank. But for the life of me, I couldn't decide if that was a good thing or a bad one.

CHAPTER ELEVEN

When I joined Kevin in the master bedroom that night, he was staring out the picture window, into the big black void of darkness. He was only wearing his t-shirt and boxer briefs—already ready for bed.

"Hey, there," I said. "How are you doing?"

"Fine," he said quietly.

I walked closer, but stopped behind him, before I was standing right next to him.

"That was pretty amazing tonight, wasn't it?" I said. "I mean, all those stories people told?"

I saw the back of his head nod.

"I didn't know any of that," I said, "about Vernie or Otto. And Ruby? How fantastic was that?"

This time he didn't nod.

That's when I knew: Kevin *was* still freaked out about the wedding, about everything that had gone wrong this weekend.

I stepped up next to him at the window. It was kind of pointless, because you still couldn't see anything at all, not even the distant lights across the bay. It was just a big black rectangle that showed the vague reflections of the room in the glass—and the mirror images of

Kevin and me. But I could tell that it was still raining outside, at least a little, with droplets gently tapping against the glass.

"It's going to be okay," I said.

He didn't say anything, but I saw his face darken in the window's reflection.

I reached out to touch him.

He pulled away ever so slightly. "How can you say that? Everything that could possibly go wrong this weekend has gone wrong. A power outage? Rabid bats? A *dead killer whale*? Seriously?"

"Everything that could possibly go wrong has not gone wrong," I said. "And didn't you hear Min? It wasn't a killer whale, it was an *orca*."

He faced me, not quite angry, but weirdly alert. "How can you *say* that?" he said again, completely ignoring my orca joke. "*Everything* has gone wrong."

"There haven't been any locusts," I said. "Or frogs. Or...huh. I can't think of any of the other ten plagues of Egypt. I can only think of two plagues? Really? How depressing is that?"

I wasn't sure if more humor was the right tact to take here, but I'd tried talking through his anxieties with him before, and I'd also tried distracting him. None of that had seemed to work, so I didn't know what else to do.

"Okay, you're right, I was wrong," Kevin said sarcastically. "It's not *everything* that could possibly go wrong. We haven't experienced the ten plagues of Egypt."

"Yeah, but now I'm curious. What *are* they?" I started looking them up on my phone.

"Lice," Kevin said quietly.

I looked up at him.

"That's one of the ten plagues," he said.

I smiled, even as I started reading my phone. "Oh! You're right, that is one. And water into blood—duh, that one's right in the movie. Then frogs, which I said. And wild animals, possibly flies. Can you believe it says that—'Wild animals, possibly flies'? They don't even know? Then diseased livestock, boils, thunderstorms of hail and fire, locusts, and death of the firstborn. Boils? Wow. I mean, technically death of the firstborn is worse, but who wants boils?"

Kevin sulked a bit, then he said, "What about the rabid bat? That could qualify as a wild animal. Or maybe it's closer to diseased livestock—it could go either way."

"Look, I'll grant you wild animals *and* diseased livestock," I said. "That's still only two plagues—two out of *ten*. You said 'everything' that could go wrong has gone wrong, but clearly you were wrong. So admit you overreacted."

Something flashed in the blackness of the window next to us—lightning out across the water, so bright that we couldn't miss it. But it happened so quickly that by the time we both turned to look at it, the sky had darkened again, and the window was exactly as black as before. A second later, thunder rumbled.

"There!" Kevin said. "Did you hear *that*?"

"The thunder?"

"Yes! That's three! We're now up to *three* of the ten plagues of Egypt!"

"What?" I said, confused.

"You literally just listed thunder as one of the ten plagues! Thirty seconds later, it starts to thunder. And you're seriously trying to tell me we're not cursed? What's next, attacking mummies?"

165

"Just to be clear," I said, "Wikipedia said thunder-storms of *hail and fire*."

"Well, maybe that's what it was!" He pursed his lips in an exaggerated kind of way.

I smiled, because now we were both in on the joke. In other words, I'd been right to use humor with Kevin. It made me happy, and a little proud, knowing that I'd finally found the right thing to say to make him feel better. (Also, and I definitely wasn't going to mention this to Kevin again, it really was nice to have *him* be the neurotic one for a change, not me.)

I turned to him and held him, and he immediately held me back, burying his face in my neck, almost even whimpering a little. He was warm, and a little damp, and his hair was wet—it smelled like his Brut shampoo. He must have taken a shower right before I got there.

"Kevin."

"What?" he said, his voice muffled by the collar of my shirt.

"Everything's going to be okay. Yes, you're right, a few things have gone wrong. But everything that hap-pened, we fixed it—*Gunnar* fixed it. If anything else goes wrong, we'll fix that too."

He nodded. "I know. It's just..."

"What?"

He pulled back and turned around, even as I kept holding him in my arms from behind. It felt a little bit like one of those paintings you see of the Madonna and the dying Jesus (but in a good way).

He didn't say anything.

"Come on," I said.

"I don't know," he said. "It's what I was saying last night. I want people to take our wedding seriously, be-cause I want people to take our *marriage* seriously. But

166

who's going to take it seriously if everything's all screwed up?"

"Yeah, but I think maybe that was wrong."

Kevin tilted his head back toward me.

"Seriously," I said, "isn't that what everyone finds so annoying about weddings? That they have to be 'perfect'? But there's no such thing as perfect, so everyone ends up getting all bent out of shape over stupid little things."

Kevin stiffened a little in my arms. "You think I'm being stupid?"

Okay, so maybe I didn't *always* say the right thing to make Kevin feel better.

"No, sorry," I said, "bad choice of words. But I think we were wrong about weddings. We were talking about how the point is for the couple to show their friends and family how much they love each other. But I'm wondering if maybe we didn't have it backward. I'm wondering if a wedding isn't more about the friends and family being able to say to the couple: we love you and we support you. That's why weddings are important."

Mostly, I was pulling this out of my ass, trying to calm Kevin down. But the more I talked, the more I realized I was onto something.

"Think about it," I said. "This was a fantastic night. First that great bachelor party, then after the power went out? All the things they said?"

Kevin nodded. "It was. We have an amazing group of friends."

"And even the whale—orca. When that happened, everyone immediately went into action to try to find us another place for the wedding."

Kevin thought about it. "You make a good point."

We unwrapped ourselves from each other, then undressed and crawled into bed. I couldn't help noticing (again) how big and soft the mattress was.

"I know I said this before," I said, "but this bed is *incredible*. What is it made of? Like, memory foam on top of kittens, on top of marshmallows, on top of actual angel hair?"

"Back home, we sleep on a two hundred dollar futon. What exactly do you expect?"

I leaned over and kissed Kevin. I felt him relaxing under me, spilling into the bed like melted candle wax.

"That's nice," he said, and I nodded.

I kissed him again. The first one had been an "I love you" kiss. This was a "Do you want to fuck?" kiss. Kevin kissed me back a third time. His kiss said, "Yes."

Full disclosure: as great as the night had been, I'd been horny ever since Nate's lap dance. I'd tried to ignore it, but ignoring horniness has never really worked for me. It was like trying to ignore an itch inside a cast—basically impossible.

Now, of course, I could finally scratch the itch.

I pulled back and, smirking, looked at Kevin. "One other important part of this weekend?" I said. "We never would've known how incredible Nate looks in a Speedo."

Kevin blushed a little. "Well, I actually *did* already know that. Roommates, remember? And, uh, I know what he looks like *out* of a Speedo."

I covered my face with my hands. "Oh, don't tell me, I don't want to know!" I peeked out through my fingers. "You know I'm not serious, right? Tell me everything. Spare no detail!"

Kevin laughed. I'd long since learned that one of the best parts about being in a same-sex relationship was sometimes discovering you both find the exact same things and people erotic. It was real a turn-on, sharing secret desires with the person you were with, and knowing he felt them too.

"What's so strange is that Nate is probably the straightest guy I know," Kevin said. "Which is a good thing, because if he hadn't been, I would've fallen madly in love with him."

"I can totally see that," I said.

"I think that's what made me so embarrassed about the striptease. It was like my fantasies of him were finally coming true, like he knew what I'd been imagining all these years."

"Except in your fantasies, it doesn't exactly stop with a striptease, huh?"

"How did you know?"

"Should I be jealous?"

"Incredibly."

I laughed and leaned in to kiss him again. He was totally relaxed now, completely knocked out of his wedding-related funk.

We kissed for a second longer, but then I pulled back.

"Something occurs to me," I said slyly.

"Huh? What?"

"This is the last time we're going to have unmarried sex. *Premarital* sex."

Kevin scrunched up his face. "We've been having sex for something like ten years now."

"Still," I said, smirking, "don't you think it's kind of hot?"

"What?"

"That we're having premarital sex! You know, what people say is so sinful and illicit."

"You're crazy. You know that, right?"

I felt the crotch of his boxer briefs, which, not surprisingly, was rock-hard and leaking precum. He'd been just as turned on by Nate's striptease as me. "Yes, *I'm* crazy," I said. I thought for a second. "We should do something different."

"Different how?"

"I don't know. Something we've never done before. Sex-wise, I mean."

"I knew what you meant. But there's *nothing* we've never done before. At least not anything that I'm *interested* in doing."

On one hand, Kevin had a point: there were plenty of things that I had no interest in ever doing sexually either. On the other hand, after tonight, I was going to be having "married" sex for the rest of my life, the kind of sex that everyone says is so boring—the kind of thing I'd been talking about with Min. I guess I couldn't say for sure I'd never have sex with anyone else ever again (Kevin and I were monogamous, and planned on *being* monogamous, but I'd listened to enough Dan Savage podcasts to know that you can't ever say never). Even so, I wasn't crazy about Kevin's attitude, especially after I'd so deftly talked away his wedding anxiety. What was that old saying about how you don't know if you like something until you try it?

"That's a fair point," I said. "Still, I'm serious. This is an important moment. The sex should be special."

"Okay, okay." He hesitated. "What does that mean exactly?"

I thought about it. "Well, for starters, it means I should take a shower too."

He gestured to the en-suite bathroom with both arms. Maybe it was my imagination, but he seemed a little impatient with me.

As I was showering, I thought to myself: *How* can *we make this sex special?* What could we do? And as I soaped myself up under the water, I started to get some interesting ideas. Yeah, technically, we'd done it all before. But not necessarily in the exact order I was planning. It was a little like a good screenplay: sure, every possible story has already been told in one form or another, but that doesn't mean *Me, Earl, and the Dying Girl* wasn't a really good movie.

I dried myself off, then flossed and brushed, and slipped into a pair of clean briefs—the closest thing I had to Nate's Speedo.

I stepped into the doorway of the bathroom, standing in my sexiest, most Nate-like pose.

I started walking toward the bed in my best possible straight-boy strut, not graceful, not polished, but confident and cocky and real.

Halfway to the bed, I heard snoring.

I stopped and stared. So much for one last night of hot, premarital sex: while I'd been taking my shower, Kevin had fallen asleep.

CHAPTER TWELVE

When I woke up the next morning, something immediately felt wrong.

For one thing, everything was quiet. It was strange
after the rain (and occasional thunder) of the night before, to not hear anything at all outside. There weren't
any other noises either. Was everyone gone? Or maybe
it was only what I'd noticed the morning before, about
how Vashon Island is so much quieter than Los Angeles.

But the world wasn't just quiet. It was still—still, but
not calm. There was something about the air, the
pressure. Was it high or low? I didn't know, but it felt
like something was going to happen, something big. It
was almost like the changing pressure was the reason I
had woken up.

That and the fact it was ten-thirty in the morning,
according to the clock. Wow, I'd slept in late, even in a
room with no curtains. I really must have been wiped
out. And it was light out, but not nearly as bright as it
had been the day before.

Kevin was gone—I was alone in bed. That was
another thing that was weird. I'd been living with Kevin

for over a year now, and we often woke up at different times, and it never felt strange. But this was our wedding weekend, so somehow it seemed odd not having him next to me.

The wedding, I thought. It was now only a few hours away.

I pulled on some clothes and made my way out into the rest of the house, but it all looked deserted. It was cold, and in the front room I could smell the lingering scent of burned candles from the night before. But I noticed that someone had cleaned up all the glasses and beer bottles, and washed the dishes in the kitchen too.

"Hello?" I said. "Is there anyone here?"

No one answered.

Somehow I knew that it wasn't like the morning before, when I was up early and I'd sensed that everyone else was still in bed. This time I could tell the house was empty. So where the hell had everyone gone? Was it the same thing that had happened to the people of Amazing? Had everyone committed ritual suicide by lining up on the porch and jumping out into the bay? Or maybe they'd been abducted by aliens. What would that be like anyway? Would they have ships with long, articulated arms like the aliens in *The War of the Worlds*? Or would they just beam them up like on *Star Trek*?

I stepped into the kitchen, and saw Min and Ruby sitting at the dining room table with their earbuds in, reading and listening to media devices.

"Oh!" I said. So much for the house being empty. It was yet another reminder that I made a really shitty Veronica Mars.

They saw me and pulled out their earbuds.

"Morning," Ruby said. "Hey, four more hours! You ready?"

I smiled. "Yeah," I said. "Uh, where is everyone?"

"They all went into town for breakfast," Min said.

I smelled coffee. It tells you how big the Amazing Inn was that I hadn't smelled it earlier.

I poured myself a cup. "Well, thanks for waiting."

"You were imagining we'd all been abducted by aliens, like at Amazing, weren't you?" Min said.

I smiled. Sometimes it can be a little embarrassing how well Min knows me.

Min and Ruby exchanged a glance, then Ruby started to stand. "Oh, hey," she said, "I've got some stuff to do."

This was sweet. They both thought Min and I might want to be alone, to talk about my feelings about the wedding. Maybe that would have been true yesterday, but I felt different about Ruby now, after what she and everyone else had said the night before.

"It's okay," I said. "You don't need to go."

She looked back at me, trying to figure out if I was only being polite.

"Really," I said.

She smiled, then half-shrugged and sank back down again.

"How are you doing?" Min said.

How *was* I doing? I had to think about that. It's (still) not that I had second thoughts or last-minute jitters about the wedding. When it came to my feelings, nothing had changed: I wanted to marry Kevin, full stop.

But I felt weird about something—something more than the atmospheric pressure—and I couldn't quite figure out what it was. It wasn't the fact that Kevin had fallen asleep before we could have hot, premarital sex— that was such a small deal it wasn't even worth mentioning to Min and Ruby.

"Well, I'm still not being neurotic in *any* way," I said, and Min smiled, and Ruby grinned too when she realized this had to be some kind of in-joke between us. "Honestly, this weekend has been fantastic. Seriously, last night? That was incredible. I felt so connected to everyone."

Min nodded and Ruby beamed. Outside a gust of wind blew, and pine needles skittered across the deck.

"But?" Min said.

"Well, ironically, the one person I've felt sort of disconnected from is Kevin," I said. "He's been preoccupied all weekend. Which makes total sense. I mean, he explained it to me Friday night, how important it is to him that the wedding go well. And then every single thing that could possibly go wrong starts to go wrong. I don't blame him, not at all. It's just ironic, like I said."

Min and Ruby nodded in sync, like those cats you see in YouTube videos.

Meanwhile, I thought about what I'd said about Kevin, and I realized it really was the truth of the weekend. It was one of those times when you don't know what you're feeling until you put it into words. The two of us played a mean Newlywed Game, but that didn't mean we were connecting, not really.

Outside, the wind blew again.

"That's weird," I said.

Min and Ruby exchanged a glance.

"What?" I said.

"Nothing," Ruby said.

"There's a windstorm coming," Min said.

A *windstorm*? Okay, now I was starting to think Kevin had been right and I'd been wrong: our wedding really was cursed.

"When?" I said.

"Um...now. They've sort've been predicting it all weekend."

So Kevin was also right and I'd been wrong about weather forecasts. The others probably hadn't brought it up with me because they didn't want to jinx things.

"But the good news is that the storm will be over this afternoon," Min said, "probably even by the time of the wedding. It's not even supposed to be that bad. So it doesn't change anything. What's the worst that could happen?"

This made me relax a little tiny bit. If the weather forecast had been right about everything else, why wouldn't they be right about this too? So what *was* the worst that could happen? We had power no matter what. And it would take a really bad storm to knock down actual trees, blocking the roads.

"I should call him," I said.

"Kevin?" Min asked, and I nodded.

I realized I hadn't turned my phone off of airplane mode (which I put it on at night). But when I did, I saw I had a voicemail from early that morning.

"Russel?" said the voice in my voicemail. "This is Angel Wells. Your caterer? I'm so, so sorry to have to say this, especially with such late notice. But our power went off last night, and it still hasn't gone back on. I've been trying to find a replacement kitchen, someone on the island with power, but I haven't been able to. I feel so terrible about this, but I'm not going to be able to provide the things we talked about."

* * *

I didn't call Kevin to tell him what Angel had said. I decided to wait until he got back from breakfast, so I could talk to him in person.

I was thinking about what I'd say to him. I was definitely going to stress what Min had said about the windstorm not being that bad. And as for the caterer, I could argue that it wasn't really a *new* disaster—that it was only the logical extension of the power outage from the night before. But even if Kevin agreed with my reasoning, I didn't see what difference that would make.

When they finally drove up, I met Kevin in the parking lot.

"I've got bad news," I said.

"The caterer canceled." He nodded. "I know, she called me too."

The others unloaded bags of groceries from the back of the car. With a grunt, Nate hoisted up a particularly heavy bag.

I looked back at Kevin. "What's going on?"

"After Angel called me, we all went to the grocery store. The power's out all over town, but the store has an emergency generator. No ice, though, so we'll need to make some here. We stopped by Angel's too, and she gave us as much food as she had, no charge. No cake, unfortunately, but we picked some up at the store. She's *really* sorry, by the way."

"But—"

"We still have three hours before the wedding. So we're going to cater the wedding ourselves."

"Really?"

Kevin nodded. I'd been expecting him to fall apart when he found out our caterer had canceled, but he didn't seem upset at all. On the contrary, he looked more focused than he had in days.

"There's one other thing," I said, wary. Even now, the air was blustery. If the windstorm hadn't officially arrived yet, it would soon enough.

Kevin nodded again, a little impatiently. "The storm. I know. It's all good, Russel. The weather says it's not going to be that bad, and it should all be over by three anyway."

With that, he turned and grabbed a couple of bags from the car.

As he started for the house, I stopped him and gave him a big long kiss. We were right in the path, so the people with the groceries had to step to one side. But we didn't care (and neither did they, judging by their smirking).

Afterward, Kevin didn't say, "What was that for?" because he knew exactly what it was for. He just smiled and headed for the house.

I looked over at Min, who had followed me outside. We didn't need to exchange any words either. We nodded to each other like two overworked waiters at a party full of entitled rich people—sharing a connection that everyone else was completely unaware of.

We had a little less than three hours to get everything ready for the wedding, but we had a fair amount to do, so everyone immediately got to work, cleaning the bathrooms, cooking the food, and rearranging the furniture.

At one point, I heard Min say, "This election is going to be the key. If the Republicans win it, they will have finally proved you really can fool most of the people most of the time. It's the ultimate triumph of ignorance over reason."

Instantly tense, I glanced over at Vernie, making canapés.

Then Vernie said, "Oh, I completely agree with you! If this group of sociopaths wins, we're all screwed. It's game over from the country and the planet."

Min and Vernie bonding over liberal politics? I totally should have seen *this* coming.

I noticed Otto over in the front room reading something on his phone. I wasn't annoyed that he'd stopped rearranging the furniture—everyone was stopping to check their phones now and then. No, it was something about the way he was standing that made me look twice, like he'd just learned either he had cancer or he'd been nominated for an Emmy.

I stepped closer.

"Is everything okay?" I asked.

He looked at me, and I saw he was crying. But I wasn't any closer to knowing if he had cancer or an Emmy nomination, because I'd probably cry if either one happened to me.

"What is it?" I said. "What's wrong?"

He wiped his eyes. "I'm an idiot, that's what's wrong."

I didn't understand so he showed me his phone. He'd received an email.

I read it:

Dear Otto Digmore:
My name is Kyle Simon, and I'm twenty-one years old. When I was five years old, our apartment caught fire and I was trapped inside. I have third

degree burns on sixty-two percent of my body, including a lot of my face. My sister was killed during the same fire. A year later, my parents divorced, and I've lived with my mom ever since. I was homeschooled for a while, then I went to high school. I dropped out, but I did get my GED. I didn't go to college, and now I work as a night watchman in an office building.

I've never really had any friends, but I like to watch TV and movies, and play video games.

I first heard you were going to be a part of *Hammered* last April. When I saw your picture, I started counting down the days until it was going to be on TV. I watched it the first night, and I know you didn't have a big part in the first episode, but I could hardly believe my eyes. After the show was over, I couldn't even talk for the rest of the night. My mom asked me what was wrong, and I said, "Nothing," and went to my room.

Since then, I've watched every episode at least five times. I've watched your web series too, a bunch of times.

This is where I should probably tell you I'm not obsessed with you, but I'm not sure I can. I am obsessed with you, but I think it's in a good way. You changed my life.

I've been meaning to write to you for a while now, but it's taken me a while to figure out exactly what I wanted to say. For a long time, even I didn't understand what I was feeling.

Discovering you has made me feel like a real person for the first time in my life. I said before that I like to watch TV and movies, and play video games, and I do, but part of me wonders if I only started doing those things because I didn't have anything else to do. Like I said, I didn't feel like a person. It never really occurred to me that I could do the things that other people did. I was a burn survivor, people stared at me, so I decided to watch TV and play video games, because it was so much simpler than anything else.

Seeing you, that started to change. It's partly that your character is out there in the world, dealing with the world. My favorite episode is "No One Wears Tighty-Whities," the one where Mike realizes you eat most of your meals in your dorm room because every time you go to the cafeteria, people stare at you. But when he encourages you to face your fears, that makes things worse. Then he shows you that you can't change that people stare at you, so you have to just own it and move on. After a while, people get bored and move on too, even when Mike wears tighty-whities on the outside of his pants.

Basically, that episode is me, except I never had a friend like Mike, so I never went to the cafeteria.

But it's not just the character on the show that has changed me. It's you. I know there's a real actor playing that character, that you're out there in the world, not caring if people stare. If you're a real person, then I can be a real person too.

Ordinarily after watching a TV show, I just watch more TV, or I go to bed. Same thing for the Internet. I read something, then I read something else.

But after watching you on TV, or reading an article about you, I don't want to stay inside. I want to go out in the world, I want to meet people.

I don't care what people say about me now. I'm not going to let them make the decision about what I get to do.

I said before that I didn't have a Mike in my life, someone encouraging me to eat in the cafeteria, but I do now. It's you. I feel sort of stupid that it took me this long in life to realize how much I was letting other people control me and my decisions, but I'm not anymore.

I don't know what I'm going to do with my life now, but for the first time, I'm asking the question. I've got a whole bunch of ideas, but this email has already gone on too long, so I won't bore you with all that.

I'm sure you get a whole bunch of emails like this, with lots of people thanking you for the difference you've made in their lives. But just in case you don't, thank you from the bottom of my heart.

Kyle Simon

P.S. I'm attaching a photo of myself, and I'm sure you know this, but that's a really big deal. For one thing, I've always hated having my picture taken. After the age of five, I think there may be ten pictures of me in my whole life. For another thing, I have never given my photo to anyone ever. You are the first.

When I finished the email, I was crying too. I looked at the photo of Kyle, and his scars were a little worse than I expected. He was staring at the camera with an expression that was somehow perfect for his letter, neither happy nor sad—an exact balance between the two.

"I'm such an idiot," Otto said, wiping his eyes.

"No," I said.

"I am! All the things I said to you yesterday about how hard my life has been? So what if people have said mean things online? I'd put up with all that stuff ten times over for an email like this."

I nodded. Truthfully, I felt like an idiot too. The day before, I'd been going on and on with Otto about how the world was a horrible place, about how people could be so awful. That was obviously all true, but it was only part of the picture. The world was also sometimes a really beautiful place. The two things were complete opposites, but somehow they were both absolutely true. Did the bad outweigh the good? Was there more bad than good in the world? Maybe, but it was exactly like Otto said: that didn't matter, because, when all was said and done, the good was so much more powerful than the bad. Who wouldn't put up with a whole boatload of shit in order to get an email as great as the one Otto had received? Like all of us, Otto had forgotten that for a while, and I had too.

Otto lowered his phone. "Sorry, I'll get back to work."

"Damn right you will," I said, "the second you finish writing that guy back."

So the windstorm raged. It was actually pretty awesome, especially since the Amazing Inn was completely surrounded by trees and looked out over the water. The branches of the fir trees shook and whipped, and we could hear needles and smaller branches hitting the roof and windows. Meanwhile, the water churned and swirled, with whorls and white caps.

But it wasn't one of those storms where you stand at the window and think, "Wow, just how bad is this going to *get*?" It was bad—make no mistake—but the weather report really had gotten it right once again. There were still even a few boats out on the water.

As for the house, it was like the opposite of a snow globe: all around us outside, everything was wild and churning, but inside everything was peaceful and calm, a little Bavarian village cheerfully preparing for the upcoming festivities. We had a strict time-limit—the wedding was at three—but everything was proceeding right on schedule.

Then Min came into the kitchen and stood there for a second, not saying anything. Somehow I knew she had something to tell me.

"What?" I said, instantly wary.

"They had to close the ferries due to the storm," she said.

"What?" I said. "But the storm isn't that bad."

"I should have known," Min said. "I guess they always close the ferries during high winds. They can't maneuver the boats into the dock. I didn't think."

I didn't know what to say. Now my head was the snow globe—the ordinary kind, with all my thoughts whirling around inside.

"Do they know when the ferries will start up again?" I asked.

"Not until the winds die down more," she said. "But there's another problem..."

"Just say it," I said.

"Well, the ferries have been stopped for hours now, and it's Sunday, so there's already a big back-up of cars who need to get back on the island."

"How big a back-up?"

She looked like she wanted to sugarcoat it somehow, but she didn't: "At least four hours."

CHAPTER THIRTEEN

"So that's it," Kevin said. "The wedding's off."

He was standing in the kitchen with us, listening to Min explain that thing about the ferries. He'd been holding it together all morning, acting perfectly calm, but the camel's back had finally broken. Now his expression was dark and brooding. Even so, his voice was surprisingly calm.

No one in the room said anything. They just watched Kevin and me—mostly me. I think they were waiting to see what I said, if I agreed with Kevin or not. Out on the deck, the vinyl cover to the barbecue flapped in the wind. Meanwhile, in my pocket, my phone vibrated—someone had texted me. I knew without looking that it was someone coming to the wedding, that they now knew that the ferry had stopped because of the windstorm and they wanted some guidance on how to react. In other words, was the wedding canceled?

Was it canceled? Kevin had already spoken—we all knew exactly what he thought—but now I guess everyone was waiting on me to confirm or deny it. To make a final decision.

"Really?" I said at last, quietly. "It doesn't have to be canceled. Does it?"

I looked around the room, at Gunnar, Otto, and Vernie, even Ruby and Nate. They all made eye contact with me, but never for long. They would look between me and Kevin, then down at the counter. I could see them thinking, saw the words on the tips of their tongues, but they hesitated. I think they all sort of sensed that this was something Kevin and I needed to decide for ourselves, and they didn't want to interfere.

Min, of course, *was* making eye contact with me, staring outright. She had an opinion too, something she thought was obvious, but it wasn't obvious to me. I'd already said we should go through with the wedding. What else did she want me to say?

"The wedding is supposed to start in an hour," Kevin said. "Even if we delay it another hour, we can't ask everyone to wait in the ferry line for four hours."

I thought about this. "The windstorm can't last forever," I said. "Once it stops, once the ferry starts running again, we have everyone park on the other side of the water, then take the ferry over here as passengers. We can all run shuttles, picking people up at the ferry dock in our cars and then driving them here."

Min relaxed a little, not quite nodding. Was that the problem—that I'd sounded so tentative before?

Everyone's eyes flicked toward Kevin, who pondered my words. It seemed to me like a pretty good plan.

"There are sixty-one guests coming," he said at last, "and the ferry dock is at least a half-hour drive from here. We don't have enough cars. It would take all afternoon. And besides, we don't know how long it'll be before the ferry starts up again."

He wasn't wrong about any of this. Now everyone looked back at me—including Kevin.

This annoyed me a little, being put on the spot. Why was it suddenly *my* responsibility to figure out a way to make the wedding work? Did Kevin not *want* to get married? And why did Kevin have the two of us discussing this in front of all our friends? Why hadn't we gone off into the master bedroom again? Our friends were great and supportive, and Kevin and I didn't have any secrets from them, but this was for the two of us to decide. As it was, we were clearly making them uncomfortable.

The silence stretched on and on, and I felt my phone vibrate again. We really did need to make a decision, if only so the people on the mainland would know what to do.

So I said, "Okay, I guess the wedding's canceled."

The second I said this, I thought, *Wait! What about Uber?* We could wait for the storm to stop, have the guests take the ferry over as passengers, but then have them take Uber or Lyft up the island to the house. But even as I thought this, I realized the whole plan was getting pretty damn complicated, especially since we'd have to communicate it via email and text to a bunch of old people who'd probably never taken Uber before.

My pocket vibrated one more time, but in the kitchen no one moved. No one was watching me now, not even to look away when I tried to make eye contact. Min looked down at the ground. This was actually worse than if they'd all been staring at me with sad, pitying eyes.

I felt like I'd failed this huge test. Seriously, it was like some evil wizard had forced me to choose between two doors, with a hot knight behind one door and a fire-breathing dragon behind the other, and I'd chosen the dragon.

Actually, this was even worse than choosing the fire-breathing dragon, because that would have been random chance—that wouldn't have had anything to do with me. This felt like it did, like I'd had an actual choice in the matter, but I'd somehow made the wrong one. I could feel the disappointment coming off my friends in waves.

But I *hadn't* made the wrong choice. Had I? For one thing, it seemed to be what Kevin wanted. And, I mean, it was wrong to ask your guests to do this long list of complicated things to get to your wedding. Wasn't it?

The wind blew again, and more pine needles skittered on the deck. The cover on the barbecue kept flapping.

Kevin turned to go.

"Kevin?" I said, but he didn't stop. He left the room like water slipping down a drain.

Finally, I met someone else's gaze. It was Gunnar.

"I guess this is one thing that even you can't help us with," I said, but he didn't say anything back, because there wasn't anything he could say.

I expected to find Kevin in the master bedroom (or ensuite bathroom), but he wasn't there. I looked around the rest of the house too, but I couldn't find him anywhere. Had he left? Where would he possibly go in the middle of a windstorm? I stepped out onto the front porch to see if he'd taken the car, but it was still parked in the lot.

The wind was crazy. The trees creaked and groaned, their branches waving around me like those big inflatable tubes you see at used car lots. It wasn't raining, but pine needles and little branches swirled all around, finally fluttering to the ground, making quiet little clicks when they landed. The air was full of the smell of pine and pitch—not surprising given all the branches and needles that had been ripped from the trees.

My phone was still vibrating off and on, but I couldn't deal with all that right now, so I flicked it off for the time being.

I looked out across the yard again. Through the swirl of the wind, I saw an opening in the trees—the road that went off to Amazing. At first I didn't think anything about it.

Then I thought, *Could Kevin have gone there? But why?*

I stepped back in the house and looked in the closet, and saw his jacket was gone. I put my jacket on too, then stepped outside. I didn't tell anyone where I was going, or even that I was leaving.

I started out across the yard. The needles still swirled around me, and the trees groaned, but I kept walking. The air was warmer than I expected, and the wind was somehow subtle too. It was like I could feel every little current on my skin.

I reached the parking lot of the Amazing Inn. There had been a layer of leaves and pine needles before, but it was so much thicker now, almost like an actual carpet. More needles whirled down around me, like snow. They felt slick under my tennis shoes.

I headed across the parking lot to the opening in the trees, the start of the road to Amazing, but everything was so thick on the ground now that I couldn't see the actual dirt at all. If I hadn't seen it before, I might not have known it was even a road.

In front of me, the trees were still swaying, their branches waving. But were they waving me forward or warning me to go back? I didn't know. Was Kevin even here? There weren't any footprints in the pine needles. And what was I going to say to him if I found him? I didn't know those things either.

I started down the road. All around me, the pine needles clicked and clacked, and the trees groaned.

We're really canceling the wedding, I thought.

Well, what choice did we have? We didn't have any realistic way to get the guests here. And what was a wedding without guests?

How did that make me feel? Weirdly, I couldn't tell. It was like I was a fire, and my emotions were smoke, and the wind was whipping them away before I even had a chance to feel them. It was a bad thing that the wedding was being canceled, I knew that much.

Around me, the forest looked different than it had before. The first time I'd been here, everything had been so still. I said it had felt like the forest was holding its breath in anticipation of what was going to happen next.

It wasn't holding its breath anymore. Now it was breathing in great big heaves, right in my face, and all around me too, making everything move that could move. Now it felt like the whole forest was in flux, like anything could happen, anything was possible.

What did it mean if Kevin and I didn't get married? Would we do it later? Try it again another weekend with our friends in the spring? But how would we afford it? And would anyone want to go through all this again? Or maybe Kevin would take this as some kind of sign, and we'd end up not getting married at all. But what would *that* mean? Would Kevin want to stay together if we weren't married? Everything was moving around me, and nothing was clear.

Now the wind shrieked through the trees, and something thrummed off in the distance—the roar of the storm overhead, maybe. A big branch crashed into the ferns to one side. I know I said before that the windstorm wasn't supposed to be strong enough to topple actual trees, but what the hell did I know? I was starting to think I'd made a mistake coming out here.

I thought about going back to the house, but I was pretty sure Kevin had come this way before me, and I needed to talk to him, even if I still didn't know what I was going to say. So I trudged forward, down the hill, the air still smelling so strongly of pine, my feet slipping on the slick carpet of needles.

Everything looked so different. Could I be lost? Had I accidentally gone down the wrong road, or not gone down a road at all? Maybe I'd wandered from the road somewhere along the way. Before, when everything was still and holding its breath, it had been possible to see through the forest, but now everything was obscured by the falling needles and swaying branches.

But no, before long I realized I'd come to the end of the road after all, to the little apron of land around the cove, the former location of the town of Amazing. I spotted the tops of the rocky ruins poking up from out of the rustling ferns. Even so, everything looked so different in the wind.

I looked up at the promontory to the left of the cove, the giant crag that faced the water. Through the wind and the needles, I saw someone standing at the top of the rock.

Kevin. He'd come to Amazing after all. I liked that I'd been able to predict it, like I'd been able to predict all the things he'd say in that bachelor party game the night before. I might have been a shitty amateur detective overall, but at least when it came to Kevin, Veronica Mars had nothing on me.

He was looking away, staring out over at the water.

There was something strange about him, something that had drawn my eyes to him even through the storm, and it took me a second to realize what it was.

All around him, everything moved: the ferns and plants and tree branches—even the tree trunks were swaying against the sky, a lot more than I would have expected. But Kevin wasn't moving at all. He stood there, legs spread, braced against the ground. He was the one solid thing in a never-ending wash of movement.

I climbed toward him, up the too-steep trail, through the plants and exposed dirt. Then I stood next to him amid those trees and ferns. I sensed that Kevin knew I was there with him, but he didn't turn to me, and I didn't turn to him. Instead, we both stared out at the sky and water—the clouds churning in front of us, the white caps in the water below us, everything a thousand shades of grey. It was somehow incredibly loud and completely quiet at exactly the same time.

We didn't speak, just kept standing there. Could we have spoken over the roar of the wind and the crash of the water? I wasn't sure, but I still didn't know what I wanted to say, and I guess Kevin didn't either. Even now, we didn't look at each other. I only saw him out of the corner of my eye—his handsome profile, his close-cropped hair barely blowing in the wind.

Why did we stand like that? For one thing, it was a pretty awesome sight, with so much to look at. The world smelled of salt and pine, fresher and cleaner than anything I'd ever known. From the waves crashing against the rocks below, a mist swirled in the air before us.

But there was something else going on. Somehow Kevin and I were a part of this incredible sight, but also apart from it, and that felt good, like it was the two of us against the storm. I'd told Min and Ruby that morning that I'd felt disconnected from Kevin all weekend long, and it was true. It had gotten worse a few minutes before, when we'd been trying to figure out what to do about the wedding. Ironically, I'd ended up agreeing with Kevin about canceling it, but now I saw that it had only pushed us further apart. That's what our friends had been reacting to with their awkward silences and lack of eye contact (and Min's *intense* eye contact): they knew that by not pushing harder for the wedding, it seemed like I had reservations about doing it at all. It was so obvious in retrospect.

Finally, still without saying a word, with the world raging all around us, we turned to each other.

I looked into Kevin's eyes, but I wasn't sure if I saw stillness or the storm—I think somehow it was both.

Then we were kissing. He tasted like the churning ocean—full of life.

As we kissed, my hands were on him, still solid, a bulwark against the storm. But his hands were on me too. We held each other up against the wind, as we also fumbled with zippers and buttons. Kevin's skin felt so smooth under his clothes, even as the skin on his hands felt wonderfully rough on me.

At the last second, we pulled away from each other, then started shucking our jackets and t-shirts, kicking off our shoes and socks, and stepping out of our pants. It wasn't like Nate's striptease—deliberately provocative. It was bolder and more matter-of-fact, nothing sly about it at all, but it was somehow even sexier.

Finally, we both slipped off our underwear and stood there facing each other on that ledge, completely naked. I expected the wind to be brisk on my skin, and it was, but it still wasn't cold. My skin had never felt so alive. It was like I was aware of every single cell. I know I said I could feel every little gust, and I still could, but now it was all over my body—even in places where I was pretty sure no wind had *ever* blown.

Kevin was beautiful, and I guess he thought I was too, because we were both fully erect. The spray of salt water from the crashing surf below washed over me, prickling my senses.

We started kissing again, pressing against each other, even as we pulled each other down. The grass was wet and soft.

Still kissing, we wrestled, but in sync, not fighting. It was more like dancing.

When we stopped, I was on top and Kevin was underneath me. Our bodies were interlocked, like a puzzle, difficult to pull apart. We were both slick with sweat and mist. I could feel his hard dick pressing up against my stomach.

I started licking his neck, tasting his skin, saltier than usual. The wind had made his skin more sensitive too, and he winced and moaned.

I worked my way down his body with my mouth. Kevin's chest was hairy but trimmed, and his nipples had always been sensitive, but were even more so now, and harder too.

My mouth dipped down, exploring his lean torso. His body was like a funnel, drawing me downward.

Kevin opened his legs for me, and I stared at him, fascinated. I said before that Kevin was the one solid thing in this whole windy forest of movement, and he still was, even more than before, but now I'm also talking about his dick. But it was different from the rest of his body too, because there was movement within, a seething pulse. This was a hardness that strained for release.

For a brief moment I wondered what would happen if someone came upon us like this, one of our friends from the Amazing Inn, or that Walker guy out hiking in the woods again. What would they think, seeing us fucking in the ferns? But this was only a fleeting thought, because I wasn't over-thinking things anymore. I didn't care if someone saw us, or maybe I even sort of liked it—was turned on by the idea of doing something so illicit.

I took Kevin in my mouth and started sucking him in open defiance of the world.

A wash of salty precum flooded my mouth, like the gush of the water against the rocks below. I sucked it in, and Kevin writhed at the intensity of the feeling of my mouth on his dick, but I held him in place with my hands, savoring the taste of him. He gently thrust toward me, and I opened wider for him.

My eyes flicked up toward his face, and I saw his lips move, knew he was moaning loudly with pleasure, but I didn't hear a thing over the churning storm.

After I released Kevin, I worked my way even farther down, still probing with my tongue, licking his balls. Above me, his granite dick still seethed.

His legs opened wider, and I didn't hesitate. I leaned forward, my mission clear, pressing my face against him. Above me, I sensed his dick still flexing, straining like the nose of jet during take-off.

As I touched him with my tongue, his whole body stretched backward, spine arched and legs planted, but still he made no sound I could hear. I surrendered to my desires, and he accepted my tongue, and together we tangled. But this did nothing to quench my lust. On the contrary, it just made it stronger, building like the wind and the storm.

We both desperately needed more, so I sat upright. My own dick was angled up from my body, wet and glistening, sticky like the pitch I could still smell seeping from trees all around me.

I crawled forward over Kevin, my chest above his torso, the two of us pressing together, touching in one single spot, but not yet joined. Everything was slick and wet—the ferns around us, the salty mist of the water— it coated us, dripped down on us, mixing with our per- spiration, my spit, and the moisture still seeping from both our dicks in quick pulses. But even so, it wasn't enough to ease the barrier between us.

I bent down to kiss him, and he kissed me back with an eagerness that surprised me even now. Now were touching in two places, and for a moment, we stayed that way, solid, both of us holding in place, the tension building.

The kiss was deep and wet, but I felt the moisture down below too—my cock still surging and dripping.

The pressure finally broke, resistance giving way to friction, and I slid into him, all in one slow glide. His body accepted and defied me in equal measure, the perfect balance.

The waves crashed and the wind howled, but all that power was nothing compared to the sensation in my dick and brain.

Now Kevin I were interlocked even more deeply than any stupid puzzle. The connection was so tight I felt like it would be impossible to move. But it wasn't impossible. I pulled back from him, feeling every inch, then forward again, into him again. He was moving too, accepting me, letting me go, but then pulling me into him again.

Now it wasn't the two of us against the storm—now there was only one, a single being, connected in a way we'd never been before. But that wasn't quite right either, because we weren't apart from the storm any more. It was raging around us, but it was a part of us too. We were all one thing, one building storm, and there was no way it was going to break, not until we had churned and howled and groaned to our heart's content, and every single drop of energy had been spent, and there was nothing more either of us had left to give.

CHAPTER FOURTEEN

I won't say that the storm broke exactly when Kevin and I were, uh, *finishing*, because that would be a little too perfect. But honestly, by the time we were done having sex, it really did seem like something in the air had changed again.

We sat in the grass amid the wet ferns, both of us still naked, staring out at the water. The water rose up in big waves, and it sloshed against the rocks below, but there were no actual whitecaps out in the channel now. The wind was calmer too, cooling the sweat on my body, but not so much that I was cold. On the contrary, the temperature was still perfect.

I'd thought the night before was going to be the last opportunity for us to have premarital sex. I guess I'd been wrong.

Boy, was I wrong! Maybe it was the unexpectedness of it all, or all the angst and emotion from the canceled wedding, or the greatness of the storm itself, but it was pretty much the best sex I'd ever had. More than that, I'd never felt so close to Kevin.

I looked out across the channel. The outline of the trees against the sky on the other side of the water was crisp and clear. The sun was just beginning to break through the streaks of the clouds, like a light bulb shining through a frayed lamp shade. Puget Sound was slowly turning from black-and-white back into color (or as colorful as it ever got on a Saturday in September).

Suddenly I sat upright.

"What is it?" Kevin asked.

"I know what happened," I said.

"Happened to what?"

"The people of Amazing!"

"The people of what?"

I explained what Min and I had been talking about all weekend long: how, years ago, there had been this little town called Amazing, and then one day all the people had disappeared. As I talked, I realized I'd never gotten around to reading that photo album of articles that Min had talked about. Yes, yes, I was a shitty amateur detective, but it didn't matter. I'd figured out the answer anyway.

"They weren't abducted by aliens," I said. "And they didn't commit mass suicide."

"So where did they go?" Kevin asked.

I looked at him and smiled. "They just left."

Kevin stared at me, not understanding.

"Amazing might have been a great place to live," I said. "There was running water, and great forests, and fresh seafood, and hey, they were a stop on the route of the Mosquito Fleet! And, I mean, look at this view. But something went wrong. Maybe the groundwater ran low, or maybe there was a fish die-off. Maybe some tragedy happened here, something they couldn't ignore. But whatever the reason, the people weren't happy. They wanted something different. So they left! There were only twenty-six people in all. That's enough to fit in a couple of boats."

"Left to go where?" Kevin asked.

"Who knows?" I turned toward Puget Sound, the actual sun visible at last, blazing and golden. "Out there somewhere. Maybe they didn't even know where they were headed. Maybe they were just taking their chances, leaving everything behind and starting fresh. I mean, why not? They thought this place was amazing—that's why they named it Amazing, right? But they were wrong. It turned out not to be amazing, not in the end. So they went out looking for it somewhere else. Because amazing isn't a place, at least not a place you can stay in for long. Nothing stays amazing forever. Amazing is a goal. If you want to live in Amazing, you have to keep looking for it. So that's where they went."

Kevin nodded, but I wasn't sure he understood completely. It didn't matter. He had his own stuff to think about, and that was okay. I wasn't sure how solid my solution to the mystery of Amazing was anyway—it probably wouldn't make a very satisfying resolution on an episode of *Veronica Mars*. But it made sense to me, at least at that moment, on that day.

Out in the channel, a boat passed by, the first one I could remember seeing since Kevin and I had climbed up onto the promontory (I was pretty sure they couldn't see us). The pine needles had long since stopped raining down around us, but I was only realizing it now.

"Let's get married," I said.

"What?" Kevin said. "How?"

"What do you mean 'how'? We go back to the Amazing Inn right now and just do it. We have everything we need: the certificate, an officiant, however many witnesses we need. Best of all, we have cake for sixty-seven people."

"Yeah, but what about the guests? I'm sure they've all gone home by now. And what about what you said last night? You said the point of a wedding was so our friends and family could show us how important we are to them."

"Maybe it is. But the people that matter the most? They're already here, back in the house. Haven't they proved themselves this weekend?"

Kevin shifted in the grass. Was he finally getting cold? I wasn't.

"What?" I said.

"Back at the house. You didn't seem all that upset when we canceled the wedding."

I thought about how to answer this. Down on the beach, seagulls screeched, excited by all the things that washed up during the storm. I couldn't help but think: *Where did the seagulls go* during *the storm?*

"That was stupid," I said. "I knew how you felt about the wedding, how you wanted it to be perfect. And I didn't even fight for it. I just let it die."

"Why? Are you having second thoughts?"

"No. Not at all."

He kept staring at me.

"*No!*" I said. "For the first time in my life, I was determined to not be neurotic about something. And I *haven't* been!"

Kevin smiled.

"But," I said, "it's true that I've been thinking about growing older." I explained how I'd somehow gotten it into my head that getting married meant the start of another stage in life—a stage where you had kids, and had problems with ear wax, and stopped having hot sex, and spent your weekends watching reruns of *House Hunters*. In other words, you did all the exact same things that a zillion other people do.

"The point is," I said, "I don't want my life to become boring. I want my life to be, well, amazing."

"Well, we might be screwed then," Kevin said, "because I actually love *House Hunters*. Or at least *House Hunters International*."

"I know!" I said. "Right?"

"But the rest of it? I don't want to be like everyone else either. I don't agree with you that having kids has to mean your life is over. For a lot of people, having kids *is* an adventure, a really interesting one." I started to say something, but Kevin interrupted me: "But I'm completely down with the fact that it's not an adventure you want to take. That's not even the point. I don't want my life to become boring, but who says it has to?"

"No one. It doesn't! That's what I've realized this weekend. As usual, it was incredibly obvious, but I was too much of an idiot to see it."

Kevin looked at me.

"Think about everything that's happened," I said. "Not just the beached orca and the rabid bat. A clothing-optional commune? That bachelor party? And don't get me started on our friends. A famous actor? Someone who's helping to build a spaceship to Mars? A guy like Gunnar who also happens to be filthy rich?" I thought for a second. "Hey, it just occurred to me that all we need is the Skipper, and we'd have the whole cast from *Gilligan's Island*." Kevin laughed, which I appreciated. "The point is, if this is the kind of stuff that happens on our wedding weekend, I can only imagine how exciting our marriage is going to be." I leaned in and lowered my voice. "And that sex we just had? I mean, my *God*."

Kevin laughed again, even as he blushed.

"But it's more than that," I went on. "Boring or amazing isn't something that happens *to* you. It's something you choose, like Vernie tried to tell me. If you surround yourself with interesting people, and if you do interesting things, your life is interesting, as simple as that. So getting married doesn't have anything to do with anything either. And if life ever *does* get boring, well, it's never too late to change it. Like the people of Amazing, you can pick up and leave."

"Leave *me*, you mean?" Kevin asked.

"We'll leave *together*," I reassured him.

Kevin's face got serious. "Screw that." We were still naked, in more ways than one, and he turned and faced me, sitting upright, sort of on one knee. "Russel Middlebrook, I promise you an amazing life. But if I turn out to be a total dud of a husband—if the last ten years have been one elaborate con to get you to marry the world's most boring person—then I give you permission to dump my ass."

At first I wasn't sure what to make of this, if I should take it seriously or if it was all a joke. But I never laughed. Instead, I turned to Kevin and said, "And I promise *you* an amazing life. And if you ever truly feel like you and I are in such different places that you can't be happy, I give you permission to leave." I thought for a second. "Although I'd appreciate it if you gave me some advance notice. Don't, like, leave me a note and take off in the middle of the night. And if I lose both my legs in an accident, please don't leave me to fester in some horrible, rat-infested, state-run facility."

"Deal," Kevin said.

We looked at each other, and it seemed like a good time to kiss, so we did.

Then we did both laugh, but it still didn't feel that much like a joke. I knew it was weird to be discussing the terms of our breaking up on our wedding day. But somehow talking about exactly what Kevin and I expected from marriage, that made the commitment we were making seem more real, more serious.

I sat back, looking out at the water again. Maybe it had to do with how hot we'd gotten from the sex or some weird warm ocean current, but I still wasn't feeling the cold. It actually felt good, invigorating, feeling the breeze on my skin. I was as clean and fresh as the wind.

"So the next question," I said. "Is this the kind of wedding you want? Going back to the Amazing Inn and reciting our vows in front of Min and the others? No other friends and family?"

He gave it some serious thought. Then he nodded and said, "I think so, yeah."

But even as he spoke, I sat upright again. Something else had occurred to me.

"Now what?" Kevin said.

"Did you send an email or text to our guests?" I said. "The people waiting in line at the ferry? Did you tell them we were canceling the wedding?"

"No, I turned off my phone."

"Oh, geez, I did too!" I fumbled for my pants, searching for my phone. "Everyone's probably so pissed off at us right now."

Kevin turned for his pants too. "Yeah, we need to tell them what's going on."

I turned on my phone, and a bunch of old texts popped up one after the other.

Yup, I thought, scanning them all. *People are annoyed.*
The last text was from Gunnar.

The wedding's back on! it read. **But don't do anything until I get back.**

I showed the text to Kevin.

"What is he talking about?" he asked.

I looked out at the water, which was much calmer now. "Maybe the ferry's running again. But even if it is, there's still the back-up. And it's too late." I looked at the clock: it was almost four o'clock. "Even with the ferry and Uber, it would take hours for everyone to get here now."

"You're right," Kevin said, but we both started pulling on our clothes anyway.

Once I was dressed, I texted Gunnar back, but of course he didn't answer.

Kevin and I climbed down the promontory, then hurried back up the road to the house. Gunnar's car wasn't in the parking lot, but the other cars were, so it wasn't like they'd all gone to pick people up at the ferry terminal.

The inside of the house felt like the waiting room at a train station, with people leaning against counters and sagging into chairs, but somehow everyone seeming impatient at the same time.

The second Kevin and I stepped inside, everyone perked up again.

"There you are!" Min said. "Where did you guys go?"

I couldn't think of a good answer to that question, so I ignored her. "What's going on?" I said. "I just got a text from Gunnar that said the wedding is back on."

"We got the same text," Otto said. "We don't know anything more than you."

I texted Gunnar again. **Where are you?** I wrote.

This time he did write back.

Almost there! he said.

I started texting him again, but then I noticed something out of the corner of my eye—more boats in the channel off-shore. At first I didn't really think anything about them. It made sense there'd be more boats out now that the storm had stopped.

They all seemed to be heading in the same direction—toward the beach below the Amazing Inn.

I turned and took a closer look.

"She'll be apples now," Nate said, standing next to me. He'd seen the boats too, even if (as usual) I didn't have any idea what his Australian slang meant.

Without a word, we all stepped out onto the deck for a better view. Three boats sailed toward us, all different sizes, none of them huge. One looked like a fishing boat, one was a small yacht, and the third was just a regular motorboat.

People crammed their decks. A bald man who looked a lot like my dad gripped the railing of the yacht. And it almost looked like my Aunt Helen standing next to him, wearing one of her trademark purple dresses.

Gunnar stood at the bow of the fishing boat. I heard him shouting to the other boats, like he was guiding them all closer to shore.

"What did he *do*?" I asked Min, who stood on the other side of me.

But of course Min didn't have any answers for me.

We all thundered down the stairs to the beach to meet Gunnar and his own Mosquito Fleet. The yacht and the fishing boat were too big to land without a dock, so Gunnar was using the motorboat as a dingy, ferrying the passengers from the other boats to shore.

There were already people on the beach when we got there—my cousins Ann, Jan, and Jane, and a couple that had lived next to my parents' house when I was growing up.

Right then, the motorboat was landing again, and Gunnar hopped out to help people down without getting their feet wet.

One of them was my mom, who turned around and saw me. "Russell!" she said. She stepped forward to hug me. "I was so worried we weren't going to make it. But Gunnar saved everything!"

Meanwhile, my dad shook Kevin's hand. "Congratulations, boys," he said.

I was literally speechless. I kept watching people climb down out of the boat, even as I spotted other faces on the two boats still farther out in the water—more relatives and family friends, and Kevin's mom and dad too.

Finally, I stepped closer to Gunnar. "How did you do this?" I asked him.

He smiled at me. "I'll tell you later," he said, then turned to continue directing the guests in from the boats.

Truthfully, it wasn't everyone who had planned to come to our wedding. Sixty-one people had RSVPed (in addition to the six people who were spending the weekend with us). Gunnar looked like he'd rounded up about thirty of them. Maybe he wasn't able to track down contact info for a lot of them, or maybe some people had already left the line at the ferry once they saw it was closed.

But now I'm nitpicking. The truth is, in a weekend full of them, Gunnar had managed to pull off the movie moment to end all movie moments.

CHAPTER FIFTEEN

The weather was still good, so we decided to hold the wedding out on the deck after all. Nate, Ruby, Gunnar, and Otto immediately went to work like little house elves, sweeping up the needles and branches, then positioning chairs from inside to go along with the chairs and benches already out there. When they finished, people somehow instinctively knew to take their seats (possibly because we were already running an hour and a half behind schedule, and everyone was, like, "Get on with it already!").

Inside the house, Min, Kevin, and I watched as the last few people sat down. We'd all cleaned up a bit, but Kevin and I weren't wearing tuxes, just nice pants and button-down shirts, and it's not like Min was wearing a robe or anything.

Finally, Min turned to us and asked, "Ready?"

We both took deep breaths, then nodded.

Together, the three of us walked out and stood in front of everyone, with the backdrop of Puget Sound off on the right. Out in the distance, the rays of the sun shone down through the clouds like stalks of golden straw.

Hey! I thought. *I was right about the weather after all!* But I was smart enough to know that five minutes before marrying someone is probably not the best time to rub their nose in how you were right and they were wrong about something.

Otto was already sitting in front of the gathering with his guitar. Right on cue—even though we hadn't *given* him a cue—he started playing and singing.

> *This time and place I'm here to say I love you*
> *This time and place is all that we can know*
> *This time and place we stand together face to face*
> *I live within your eyes this time and place*

As I listened to Otto sing, I remembered how impressed I'd been by his musical talent all those years ago at summer camp. But honestly, when I'd asked him to sing at our wedding, I'd forgotten how good he was. It was funny how one of the first things I'd noticed about him was that he was a natural-born performer, and now, nine years later, he was a famous actor.

> *Some people say the past is like a river*
> *That sweeps us forth into who we're supposed to be*
> *But as for me, the past is gone forever*
> *So don't come talkin' to me 'bout destiny*

I didn't recognize the song Otto was singing. Then I remembered he was a songwriter too, and I realized he must have written the song for us, for our wedding.

> *Other people say our future's in the heavens*
> *And the stars converge into some grand design*

But as for me, I don't need no lucky sevens
And I don't need spinning moons to make up my mind

As Otto sang, I looked out at the faces of the crowd—Nate and Ruby, sitting together, and Gunnar, grinning like he'd just discovered a new animal phylum. Vernie was seated with an older man, someone it took me a second to place: Walker, the guy Min and I had met in the ruins of Amazing the day before. Did she have a date or what?

Leave the past alone
Let the future be
'Cause this time and place
You're here with me

This time and place I'm here to say I love you
This time and place is all that we can know
This time and place we stand together face to face
I live within your eyes this time and place
I'm really glad we're here ... this time and place

When Otto finished, I could tell people were impressed with him, and probably also flattered that a TV star had deigned to sing for them. I wanted people to applaud, but it was a wedding, so no one did.

Min stepped forward. "Welcome to the wedding of Kevin and Russel," she said. "My name is Min, and we're happy you finally made it. You all passed the test!"

Everyone laughed—*really* laughed—and I realized that picking Min to be our officiant had been another great call on Kevin's and my part.

"My mother is annoyingly wise," Min said to the crowd. "And when I was eleven years old, I asked her what it means to be married. She thought for a second, then called into the other room and asked if my father would bring her magazine into the kitchen for her. A second later, my father trundled into the room with her magazine, kissed her on the top of the head, then left again. When he was gone, I said to my mom, 'Well?' 'Well, what?' my mother said as she casually paged through her magazine. 'I asked you a question about marriage,' I said, 'but you didn't answer it!' And she said, 'Oh, I answered it.'"

The crowd was one collective knowing grin.

"I thought about what my mother had done, the point she was trying to make," Min said. "Finally I asked her, 'But what if he'd told you to get your own darn magazine? What if he'd stomped into the kitchen with a scowl and thrown the magazine down onto the table?' And of course my mom smiled and said, 'That would have been what it means to be married too.'"

Now everyone on that deck laughed, including me.

"So Kevin and Russel?" Min said, turning to us. "I'm sure you both already know that no marriage is perfect. But my wedding wish for you is that you have very little scowling and magazine-throwing, but lots and lots of head-kissing."

I smiled at her, then at Kevin too. Min wasn't a touchy-feely type, but she sure knew how to rock a wedding anecdote (even Vernie looked impressed). It was interesting how, after everything that could possibly go wrong with our wedding had gone wrong, now everything was suddenly going right. But I guess there's some kind of lesson there, something about how we spend most of our lives getting all bent out of shape about things that don't matter in the least.

Min faced the crowd again and said, "Russel and Kevin have both written their own wedding vows."

We have? I thought. This was what I'd told Min weeks ago, and I'd even jotted a few things down somewhere. I'd been planning to finalize my vows over the weekend, but I'd been so distracted by everything that had gone on that I'd forgotten all about it. It's not like we'd thought to do a rehearsal. As a result, I had no idea what I was going to say.

I looked out at the crowd again, hoping to be filled with inspiration. But whereas before I'd seen the smiling faces of Gunnar and Vernie, now I saw the mugs of everyone else: my parents, my uncle Joe, and Mr. Ingram, one of my dad's co-workers. They were smiling too—well, Mr. Ingram wasn't, and he even looked down at his watch—but it wasn't the same. My mom had a nervous twitch. Meanwhile, my dad was smiling *too* broadly. Maybe it was the gay thing. Had my Aunt Helen ever been to a same-sex wedding? Had she ever seen two men kiss, even on TV? Maybe she had, but none of these people had ever seen me kiss Kevin, not even my parents.

So much for everything going right in the ceremony, I thought.

Kevin must have seen the panic in my eyes, because he immediately pulled out a three-by-five card, indicating that he'd go first. As nervous as I was, I couldn't help noticing how damn handsome he looked in his button-down shirt, and how he had such gentle eyes. But before he even glanced at his prepared card, Kevin lowered it. He was going off-book too.

"Russel," he said, "all weekend long I've been worried that something would go wrong at our wedding, and you told me not to worry. Well, *everything* went wrong. So basically I was right and you were wrong."

People laughed, and I thought, *So much for not rubbing your groom's nose in his mistakes in the middle of a wedding!* But at the same time, I was pretty sure he was going somewhere with this.

"Except I *wasn't* right," Kevin went on, "because this wedding is perfect exactly the way it is. The only way our wedding wouldn't be perfect is if it didn't happen. And now that it's happening, I have a chance to tell you how much I love you, and how much I want to spend my life with you. Earlier today, you said you wanted an amazing life. This is my vow to you: I promise to do everything in my power to give you one."

What Kevin had said was really sweet, and he still looked damn handsome, so I smiled. Unfortunately, I still had no idea what I was going to say in return—despite the fact that every single person on the deck was now staring at me, including Kevin.

I thought about the conversations Min and I had been having this weekend, and the talk that Kevin and I had over in Amazing. What had all that been about? Something about getting older? No, wait, maybe it had to do with kids. Or *House Hunters*? Suddenly I couldn't remember.

I've said all along that my concerns about the wedding were just little quibbles, barely worth mentioning—nothing neurotic, and definitely not anything approaching cold feet. But even I didn't know that for sure. Maybe I'd been lying to myself.

Now I *did* know for sure.

I guess my view of weddings had changed one more time: it wasn't about us saying anything to our friends and family, or our friends and family saying something to us. It was about that moment when I realized—finally and for sure—exactly what I felt for Kevin, and what he and I meant to each other.

Or—and maybe this is the real truth—our wedding was about all these things together, all of them at the same time.

Given how I was having this moment of clarity, and given that the wedding had all seemed to come together at the last moment—the sun came out! Gunnar arrived with the guests! Min's wedding anecdote was hilarious!—I expected to open my mouth and have the perfect words flow right out of me.

But I still couldn't figure out how to put it all into words.

So instead, I leaned forward and gave Kevin a kiss on the head. Then I said, "Here's *my* vow: a lifetime of that."

It was only after I did it I realized that for a person who had a tendency to over-think things, it actually *was* the perfect thing to say.

Appreciating the nod to her story, Min immediately perked up. "Hey, that works for me!"

"Me too," Kevin said, his smiling face somehow even more handsome than before.

"And so," Min went on, "by the power invested in me not by God or government, but by Kevin and Russel themselves, I now pronounce you married." She looked between us, then winked and added, "Go to it, boys."

Kevin and I leaned in for a kiss, deep and lingering, my Aunt Helen be damned.

At that, Min held her arms out around us and said to the gathering, "I now present two husbands, Kevin Land and Russel Middlebrook!"

As if there was ever any doubt. I told you at the beginning I was a reliable narrator. It was your own damn fault if you didn't believe me.

CHAPTER SIXTEEN

After the ceremony, Kevin and I talked to our parents first, mostly due to the whole having-given-birth-to-us thing. They said all the right things, and I was actually glad they'd come. We mingled with the other guests too. My Aunt Helen couldn't wait to kiss me on the cheek—and she had actual tears in her eyes. How great is that?

While Kevin and I accepted the congratulations of the crowd, our close friends went into house elf mode again, pouring drinks and ushering everyone into the area with the food spread.

At one point, I passed Nate who was popping another bottle of champagne.

He stopped me to say, "That was really great. Especially the kiss on the head. I think this might be the best wedding I've ever been to."

"Really?" I said, blushing, even as I realized it was one of the first things Nate had said all weekend that I'd understood perfectly right from the start.

* * *

Not long after, I pulled Otto aside, and I was about to tell him how great his song had been, but he spoke first.

"That was fantastic!" he said. "Russel, I'm so happy for you. Seriously, I spent the whole ceremony with this stupid grin on my face. Thanks so much for inviting me."

"Are you kidding?" I said. "You *had* to be here." I wanted to say more, to tell him how important he was to me, but once again I couldn't find the right words. After all, Otto was my ex, and in certain alternate realities, I could see marrying him and not Kevin. In fact, I almost said to him, "I hope you know you're going to be married someday too," but I quickly realized how condescending that sounded. Besides, I hated when a person had some life event, a marriage or a childbirth, and they suddenly acted like the universe had bestowed this great wisdom onto them.

"Oh! I loved your song!" I said, remembering. "You wrote it, didn't you? I'm so flattered."

His face brightened. "You really liked it?"

"Oh, *yeah*."

He nodded. "Yeah, Lady Gaga liked it a lot too."

"You played your song for—?" I started to say, but then I saw the expression on his face. He was bullshitting me, so I swatted him on the arm. (At least I *think* he was bullshitting me. Maybe he'd told the truth, but decided he didn't want to make me feel bad on my wedding day.)

"Oh, hey, guess what?" he said. "I already heard back from the guy who wrote to me."

"Really? What did he say?"

"He couldn't believe I wrote him. Which always seems so strange to me. Are there really people who wouldn't respond to an email like that?"

"I know, it's crazy."

Neither of us said anything for a second.

"Otto?" I said.

"Yeah?"

But once again, I couldn't find the right words, so I hugged him instead, hard and long. Not being a hugger, I guess I didn't understand that sometimes this was a way to say things you couldn't quite put into words.

"Congratulations!" Vernie said to me, out on the deck. "That was exactly as wonderful as I knew it would be."

"Thanks," I said. I nodded at Walker, inside getting food. "And what's the story there?"

"I met him out walking this morning. And..."

"What?"

"Well, I decided you were right. My life doesn't have to end just because I'm sixty-eight years old."

"Vernie, you're seventy-four."

She laughed. "Yeah, but he doesn't know that!" She leaned in close. "You also might have been right about the other thing. We've got a date tonight."

"What—?" Then I realized she was talking about getting laid, and I blushed. "That's fantastic, Vernie. I'm so happy for you."

"Oh, please, it's the oldest story in the book. The mentor thinks she has all the answers, but it turns out she learns something from her protégé? How many times have we seen *that* story? What a cliché!"

"Speaking of screenplay ideas," I said, "I think I know what I'm going to write next."

"Do tell."

"Well, I'm going to write about this weekend. About two guys getting married, and how they invite all their closest friends to spend the days before with them, getting everything ready."

"Really?"

"Yeah, but halfway through the weekend, aliens invade."

"Are you serious?"

"Totally! I mean, has there *ever* been a gay, alien-invasion movie?"

Vernie smiled. "But I thought the whole point was to write a low-budget script. Aliens mean special effects, which are expensive."

"Yup! I changed my mind. I decided to write the movie I wanted to write, to hell with the cost."

Vernie smiled. "Go big or go home?"

"Exactly! I'm writing movies, right? So let's write some *movies*."

"But with subversive gay undertones."

"Well, I mean, it *is* me," I said. "Anyway, it sounds like we both figured a few things out these last few days."

"Oh, please! Life isn't like in the movies. People don't solve all of their problems over the course of a single weekend."

"Of course not!" I said, and we both stood there grinning like the fools we were.

Later, I found Min. "You were absolutely terrific," I said.

"Thanks," she said. "It was truly an honor."

At that, both our eyes fell on Ruby, over in the kitchen serving cake.

"She's really great," I said.

"She is, isn't she? For the first time in a long time, I can actually see myself getting married one day. Maybe not any time soon, but someday. Can you believe it? Me, the person who is so terrible at relationships?"

"I *can* believe it. Oh, hey, I didn't tell you. I figured out what happened to the people of Amazing."

"Oh?" she said. "This should be good."

I told her my theory, and she thought about it.

"So Amazing isn't a place, it's a state of mind?"

"Exactly."

She thought for a second, then nodded. "I like it!"

We both stood there, looking out at the crowd.

"Min?" I said. "Thanks for everything."

"Anytime."

I turned to her. "No. I mean *everything*."

"Anytime," she said again, but this time it meant something altogether different.

I still wasn't a hugger, but in Min's case, I decided to make another exception.

Later still, Gunnar came to me and handed me an envelope.

"What's this?" I asked.

"Open it," he said.

So I did. It was a check for twenty thousand dollars.

"What in the—?"

"It's my wedding gift to you guys."

"Gunnar! You already gave us a wedding gift! Remember? You said you were going to make sure nothing got in the way of our wedding. And you did! You were absolutely great. I have no idea how you did the things you did, but you did them anyway."

"Craig's List."

"What?"

"That's how I got rid of the orca. Plus, a little basic physics. I hired someone with a big boat. That's also how I found the boats to bring everybody here for the wedding. Hey, it's the sharing economy, right? But I figured out how to operate the generator on my own."

"*Gunnar!*" I said, but at least I was smiling when I said this.

"What?" he said with his usual cluelessness.

"The point *is*," I said, "you already *did* all those things. *That* was your wedding gift to us, and it was the best gift anyone could have possibly given. You don't need to give us twenty thousand dollars!"

He shrugged. "I'm selling my houseboat. Do you have any idea how insane the Seattle real estate market has been these last few years? I'm going to make seven hundred thousand dollars. Oh, hey, I also signed on with the crew of this research vessel for six months. We're going to be studying penguins in Tierra del Fuego. Word is we'll be heading to Antarctica too."

"Really? That's fantastic! But wait, go back. I don't *care* if you sold your houseboat. We still can't take twenty thousand dollars of your money."

"Sure, you can. Didn't you tell me you couldn't afford a honeymoon? That you were disappointed about what a lame start that was for your marriage?"

I had told Gunnar that, weeks ago. But that was before everything that had happened this weekend.

"Gunnar—"

"Look, Russ, you can either take it now, or I'll hack into your checking account and deposit it without you and Kevin knowing. So which is it gonna be?"

Clearly, I really did have the world's best friends.

By early evening, the ferries were running again. This time, we used Uber, and all our parents and family and friends left. Min, Gunnar, Otto, Vernie, Ruby, and Nate stayed behind to help Kevin and me clean up. After that, Min signed our wedding certificate, and Nate and Gunnar acted as our witnesses, and we all had another toast of champagne, and Kevin and I were officially married.

By then, everyone else had to leave, to get back to their real lives (and Vernie had her date). So after some tearful goodbyes, and even a few more hugs, everyone went their separate ways.

Kevin and I had our own plane trip back to Los Angeles, but not until the following afternoon, so he and I spent that last night by ourselves at the Amazing Inn.

When the last person was finally gone, he turned to me and said, "Well?"

Once again, I was at a loss for words. What could I say? It was a little like with Otto and fame: the weekend had been simultaneously far worse than I had ever imagined (with all the things that had gone wrong), and also far better (the way everything had worked out in the end).

"Yeah," Kevin said, reading my expression and nodding, "I know."

I looked around the house, which was sparkling clean but sterile and empty now, and that made me sad. When we'd rented this place, we'd been incredibly stressed out about how expensive it was, worried how we'd pay for the whole wedding. With Gunnar's check, we didn't need to panic about money anymore, at least for a little while.

"Do you feel any different?" he asked me. "Now that we're married?"

I concentrated like I was trying to feel the bones inside my body. Finally, I said, "I feel good—really, really good. Well, I'm sad that everyone is gone. But I'm happy that I'm here with you. About us, no, I don't feel any different. Not at *all*, in fact. I feel exactly the same about you that I did before. That I have for a long, long time. I'm really glad we got married, and it did help clarify a few things in my mind. But it's funny. I think mostly what it did was acknowledge the obvious."

He laughed. "That about sums it up, doesn't it?"

Did everyone feel this way after getting married? It sort of went against the school of thought that said that getting married was a Really Big Deal, and everyone needs to take it Really, Really Seriously.

But that's the thing. I don't think it's bad acknowledging that commitment is something different from marriage. Sometimes the two things go together, but not always, because commitment is what happens on the inside, what you feel, and it doesn't necessarily have anything to do with the words you say, or your signature on a piece of paper.

Anyway, it was nice to know I'd felt a really strong commitment to Kevin for a while now, because I was pretty sure it meant I'd married the right guy.

* * *

Later, as Kevin and I were getting ready to go to sleep, I said to him, "You know, I really like this bed."

"Yeah, me too," he said. "It's great."

"I'm getting tired of our futon. Thanks to Gunnar, we can afford a new bed now."

Kevin thought about it. "I'm not sure I can handle that. Getting married and buying a grown-up bed, both in the same year?"

"Is that what it would be? A grown-up bed? A sign that we've entered the next stage of our lives?"

"Wouldn't it?"

I thought about it. "No," I said at last. "I think it just means I'm tired of sleeping on a damn futon!"

We both laughed.

We flossed, and brushed our teeth, and washed and moisturized our faces—all the things we always did before going to bed at night. At one point, I realized that this was the first time we'd done those things as a married couple, but a second later, I thought, *So what?*

We had sex that night too—our first sex as a married couple, but I'm not sure either of us was even aware that it *was* our first married sex. As for the sex itself, it wasn't nearly as good as the sex in the woods that morning (not even *close*), but it was still pretty fun.

Kevin fell asleep right after, but I stayed awake for a bit, spooning him from behind. I gazed over at the big window with no curtains, but it looked different with the lights off, because now I could see outside: the outline of tree trunks with the stars beyond.

I remembered what I'd decided about the people of Amazing—about how they didn't like the way things were in their town, so they'd up and left. They'd gone off over the horizon, to find a better place to be. They'd learned you couldn't live in a place called Amazing, not for long anyway, because it always had a way of slipping away from you.

But as I lay there in bed, I wondered if that was true.

I thought about everything that had happened to me since I first met Kevin Land, back in middle school or high school, however you calculated it. I thought about all the people I'd encountered, the things I'd done. Some of it had been good, some of it bad, and a lot of it had been pretty damn interesting, at least to me.

I held Kevin tighter in the dark, feeling his body against mine—the hardness of his muscles, the smoothness of his skin. He was so warm, like cuddling a summer day, and he smelled so good—this perfect combination of the cocky, confident boy he'd seemed to be in high school and the gentle, sensitive man I now knew he was.

That's when I thought: maybe Amazing *wasn't* something over the horizon, something off in the future. Maybe it wasn't about the beauty of the struggle either, appreciating the journey *to* the destination.

No, maybe Amazing was all around me, a constant thing, part of every molecule of matter, present in every second of every day. But for some reason, I couldn't see it, except in glimpses, except in moments like this one, lying in bed in the dark with Kevin.

It was a nice thought, the idea that the place I was going to was the place where I already was.

I tried to cling to that thought, even as I held tightly to Kevin. But it had been a long day and I was exhausted, and before I knew it, I drifted off to sleep.

The story continues in:
The Otto Digmore Difference,
the start of a new series about Russel's friend Otto.

ALSO BY BRENT HARTINGER

ABOUT THE AUTHOR

Brent Hartinger is an author and screenwriter. *Geography Club*, the book in which Russel Middlebrook first appears (as a teenager), is also a successful stage play and a feature film co-starring Scott Bakula. It's now being adapted as a television series.

Brent's other books include the gay teen mystery/thriller *Three Truths and a Lie*, which was nominated for an Edgar Award.

As a screenwriter, Brent currently has four film projects in development.

In 1990, Brent helped found the world's third LGBT teen support group, in his hometown of Tacoma, Washington. In 2005, he co-founded the entertainment website AfterElton.com, which was sold to MTV/Viacom in 2006. He currently co-hosts a podcast called Media Carnivores from his home in Seattle, where he lives with his husband, writer Michael Jensen. Read more by and about Brent, or contact him at brenthartinger.com.

ACKNOWLEDGEMENTS

Thanks, as always, to my husband Michael Jensen, my editor Stephen Fraser, and my agent Jennifer De Chiara.

Thanks also to Philip Malaczewski for continuing to create great book jackets (this one's my favorite so far).

I had a great time co-writing a real-life version of Otto's song, "This Time and Place," with my friend Danny Oryshchyn, and another friend, Jeremy Ward, did a terrific job helping me record and sing it. Look for the video online (but keep your expectations low: I'm a writer, not a singer!).

Early readers who generously contributed their time and extremely helpful opinions on this book include Matt Carrillo, Paul Chiocco, Nate Edmunds, Erik Hanberg, Michael Higgins, Wes Jamison, Brian Katcher, Bill Konigsberg, Brad Lane, Nate Leslie, Mark MacDougal, Joe Muscolo, Tim O'Leary, Peter Orem, Lucas Orosco, Robin Reardon, Tim Sandusky, Lais Santos, R.J. Seeley, Gregory Taylor, and Christopher Udal.